SPIDER MORGAN'S SECRET

When the little crook, Spider Morgan, bursts into Victoria Lincoln's office, he's being followed — and his life is in danger. She lets him hide in her office strongroom and soon two bogus police officials pay a call. They question Victoria about Spider, but she sends them on their way. The next day she learns that Morgan has been beaten senseless and left in a coma. Then after her office is burgled — Victoria and her staff are being followed . . .

JOHN RUSSELL FEARN
Edited by
PHILIP HARBOTTLE

◆

SPIDER MORGAN'S SECRET

Complete and Unabridged

LINFORD
Leicester

First published in Great Britain

First Linford Edition
published 2011

British Library CIP Data

Fearn, John Russell, *1908 – 1960*.
Spider Morgan's secret. - -
(Linford mystery library)
1. Suspense fiction.
2. Large type books.
I. Title II. Series
823.9'12–dc22

ISBN 978–1–4448–0772–1

Published by

hing)
iire

d.

ain by
:ornwall

paper

1

SPIDER MORGAN'S SECRET

1

Sanctuary

He was a wizened, dried-up little man, with close-set eyes that glittered with evil.

His every movement was furtive, from his shuffling gait to the rapid glance over his shoulder, which he made at almost every other step.

Spider Morgan was being shadowed — and he knew it; he also knew that they who followed him were ruthless in their methods and would stop at nothing to secure the little package that was thrust down deep into the pocket of his shabby, greasy jacket, where his right hand never let go of it for the fraction of a second.

Quickly and agitatedly, the little man crossed from one side of Regent Street to the other. If his luck held good for another ten minutes or so he might even yet reach the rabbit warren of Soho and so be able to dive to cover in one or other of a score of unsavoury bolt holes — but, even in mid-street, Spider cast that furtive glance over his shoulder and knew that his pursuers were closing in with stubborn relentlessness.

Reaching the pavement on the north side of the street, Spider suddenly realized that, for a moment, a press of traffic hid him from view and, heedless of where he went now, the little man shot through an open doorway in search of sanctuary.

His beady, darting eyes took in the details of his surroundings automatically. He realized that he had passed the portals of Kingswood House, a block of offices that stretched full length across the showrooms of a world-famous Regent Street store. A uniformed commissionaire was busy on a telephone switchboard in a tiny glass-enclosed office; a smart lift-boy was just entering the gates of the elevator, the buzzer of which had just sounded through the entrance hall.

Spider Morgan saw his chance and leapt at it. The commissionaire was fully occupied; the lift was now out of sight. Noiselessly the little man sped towards the broad stone staircase and scuttled upwards as if Death were at his heels — as it most certainly was.

The fugitive did not see the painted name upon the glass-panelled door that confronted him as he reached the floor above — or if he did it conveyed nothing to him except that here, perhaps, was the sanctuary he craved.

He heard the steady tapping of a typewriter as he turned the door-handle and glided silently inside. For a moment he paused with his back against the door — and breathed a little more freely, feeling that his audacity had gained him slight respite. He knew, however, that he had no time to lose.

His furtive eyes darted round the office in which he now found himself — and he straightened a little out of his habitual cringe as he discovered that the only occupants of the room were two girls — two young girls both deeply absorbed in their tasks.

The girl at the typewriter suddenly

paused in her work and looked across at her companion.

'Isn't it silly, Pam?' she said with a slightly embarrassed little laugh. 'I've completely forgotten how to spell — *Oh!*'

The exclamation was uttered sharply and in a higher key. The speaker had just caught sight of Spider Morgan furtively approaching the centre of the room.

The other girl turned quickly and saw the little man almost in the same instant.

'Y-yes? Did — did you want someone?' she asked, uncertainly. 'Have you — '

'Now — now! Don't get alarmed, young ladies!' cut in Spider, quickly. 'Y'see, I — I've been taken a bit queer — just wanted a sit down a minute and rest, see? No call for you to get excited. I didn't mean no 'arm.'

Feeling that he had the situation well in hand, Spider edged towards the closed door of an inner office.

Maybe if he could get in there out of sight he might even yet give his pursuers the slip. These 'kids', as he mentally classified the two girls, wouldn't give him any trouble. He could handle them all right — and several more like them. Maybe, however, he'd better throw a bit of a scare into them — just to let them see they couldn't trifle with him

Clutching the little package in his pocket tightly and thus making a bulge that might suggest a deadly weapon to an imaginative mind, Spider summoned up a look that was meant to appear menacing.

'Just you keep quiet — and stay right where you are!' he muttered, fiercely. 'Hold your tongues — and no 'arm will come to yer, see?'

Backing slowly towards the door, his left hand outstretched as he groped for the handle, the little man glared menacingly at the two girls who sat motionlessly watching him.

Then, so quickly and so suddenly that Spider had no chance to make the slightest move, he found his left wrist gripped in a cool, firm hand; a quick twist and his arm was up his back and there he was, helplessly locked in an arm-hold from which he knew there was no escape short of breaking a bone.

'All right, guv'nor! No offence!' Spider

began to whine — and then he found himself spun round to face his captor who still maintained that locking grip.

It was no man who held the intruder so firmly, however. Spider found himself looking into the hard, suspicious eyes of a very capable young woman who showed not the slightest intention of being intimidated — nor of loosening her hold.

'Give me a hand here, Carol, please!' said the captor. 'Pamela — just stand by to 'phone for assistance — should we need it — not that I think we will, however!'

'Yes, Miss Lincoln!' replied the two girls in chorus and the fair-haired Caroline Gerrard hurried forward into the inner office where Victoria Lincoln, the famous detective, had now urged her captive.

'Search him for a gun, Carol, my dear,' said Victoria, quietly. 'He seems to be very fond of something in his right-hand pocket.'

Deftly and expertly Carol frisked the crestfallen Spider but quickly reported that the intruder did not appear to be armed.

Satisfied, Victoria released her grip, stepped back a pace and, with her hands behind her back, coldly surveyed the furtive little man.

'Who are you — and just what do you mean by breaking into my office like this?' the detective demanded. 'I suppose it's money you're after — thought you had an easy break with my secretary and my young assistant, eh? Well, anything to say before I 'phone the police?'

'Lumme! Have a 'eart, lady!' whined Spider. 'I never come 'ere to steal — straight, I didn't! I — I'm in trouble. I — I was being tailed, see? By a couple of tough eggs who ain't got no cause to like me, see? I — I only come in 'ere to 'ide. That's straight up.'

'One jump ahead of the police, eh?'' said Miss Lincoln, tartly. 'Well, it won't be the first time I've given them a helping hand. Better tell Pamela to dial Whitehall 1212, Carol. We — '

'Just a minute, lady!' cut in Spider Morgan, anxiously. 'I ain't in trouble with the 'cops — not just now, I ain't. Ring up the Yard and ask 'em if you like. They know me there — but I ain't wanted by them for anything — straight up, I ain't. I only came 'ere to — to get away from — from these other guys. I — I reckon they'll kill me if they lay hold o' me now — see?'

Victoria Lincoln studied him closely for a moment and then seemed to come to a decision.

'What's your name?' she demanded. 'And just why did you come to my office to seek sanctuary?'

'The name's Morgan — at the moment — Bill Morgan,' said the little man, eagerly. 'At the Yard they know me as 'Spider', see? I didn't come 'ere to this particular office for any reason — except that it was the first one — and the nearest.'

'Then you don't know who I am — or anything about me?' pressed Victoria.

Spider shook his head emphatically and Victoria took a business card from her desk and handed it to her unwelcome visitor.

'Victoria Lincoln, Private Investigator',' Spider read aloud. 'Lumme, lady! I sure didn't know I was coming into the office of a lady 'tec — take my oath on it and — '

Spider paused and his head went on one side like that of a terrier that has heard a suspicious footstep.

'Someone comin'!' he muttered. 'It's them, lady! 'Ide me! 'Ide me for the love of Mike! They'n kill me if they lay hands on me now!'

Victoria eyed him with severe disfavour.

'I'll hide you, Morgan,' she said, quickly. 'Not that I care much what happens to evil little crooks like you — but because I don't want any violence to take place on my premises — murder is such a messy business at times. Carol — take him into the Records Room — and lock the door. Then come back here — quickly, my dear!'

So Carol Gerrard hustled the anxious Spider Morgan back into the outer office and then through the steel door of the Records Room, which was really a commodious safe in which the famous detective kept her priceless record files. In a few moments Victoria's young and pretty assistant had locked the heavy door and was returning to the inner office when two men bustled briskly into the room.

'Ah, good morning! Good morning!' one of them said, breezily. 'Miss Lincoln? Miss Victoria Lincoln — is she engaged at the moment?'

'Miss Lincoln is not engaged at the moment,' said Carol, controlling her excitement. 'Unless you have an appointment, however, I'm — '

'Must see her, my dear!' cut in the other newcomer, familiarly. 'Urgent police matter, you understand?'

'If you'll give me your names I'll see if Miss Lincoln can spare time for a consultation,' said Carol. 'She — '

'Names don't matter, my girl!' said the first man, hurriedly. 'Just tell her we're from the police — on official business.'

Carol tapped on the inner office door and entered. She was absent only a few seconds and when she returned she beckoned the callers to enter.

Seated at her desk Victoria Lincoln eyed the two men in a manner that enabled her to register a mental description of both of them. Then she smiled disarmingly and bade them both be seated. Carol turned to go but the detective stopped her with a gesture and signed to her to pick up a pencil and prepare to take notes.

'I understand you are from the police, gentlemen,' said Victoria, in businesslike tones. 'Just what can I do for you?'

'We're on the track of a notorious little crook known as Morgan, Spider Morgan, Miss Lincoln,' said one of the callers, quickly. 'We have reason to believe that he is — or has been — in this building. Can you give us any information, please? Has he been here?'

'Before I answer any questions,' said Victoria, slowly, 'hadn't you better identify yourselves, gentlemen? I'd like to see your credentials, if you don't mind?'

'We didn't come here to waste time!' blustered the smaller of the two callers. 'You answer questions — or else — '

'Something new for police officers to utter threats, isn't it?' said Victoria, cuttingly. 'I'm sorry, gentlemen. I don't do business with strangers.'

'Pardon me, Miss Lincoln,' said the second man tugging at his companion's sleeve, 'my colleague is rather hasty. He so nearly laid hands on Morgan this morning and he's somewhat peeved at losing sight of him. Let me introduce ourselves. I am Detective-sergeant Worsely; this is Detective-inspector Brown. We're both C.I.D., Devon County Constabulary — and we need this man Morgan rather badly. Now if you can give us any information at all we'll be glad of it. We — '

He paused and frowned slightly. Victoria Lincoln was apparently paying no heed whatever to him. Quickly and quietly she had dialled a number on her desk telephone and now placed the receiver to her ear.

'Scotland Yard?' she said. 'Victoria Lincoln here, Inspector Beesley, Liaison Department, please. Oh — hello, Inspector. Yes, that's right. I have two men here claiming to be C.I.D. men from Devon

C.C. A Sergeant Worsely and an Inspector Brown. Will you check on them, please? They don't appear to possess warrant cards and — '

The detective ceased speaking. With muttered oaths the two alleged detectives had turned on their heels and hurried away. The outer office door banged behind them and with a rather cynical laugh Victoria replaced the receiver and turned to her young assistant.

'Take a peep and make sure they've left the premises. Carol,' she said. 'Never before have I seen such obvious frauds as those two! Policemen, indeed! Anything they know about the police force has been learned from the wrong side of the law, I know!'

Carol hurried away to return a few minutes later to report that she had observed the two men enter a car that had been waiting outside in Regent Street and this had then hurriedly driven off towards Piccadilly.

'Did the Yard confirm your suspicions, Vicky?' Carol asked with a smile when she had made her report. 'Did they — '

'I didn't bother the Yard, my dear,' said Victoria.' I spoke only to Pamela in the outer office — but the ruse was sufficient to prove my suspicions. I think we can produce our scared little Spider Morgan now and tell him it's safe for him to scuttle off to some more permanent hiding place.'

Spider Morgan seemed a little more at ease when once again he faced Victoria Lincoln in her office.

'They've gone, eh, lady?' he said, with a rather sheepish grin. 'Much obliged to yer I'm sure. Hope to do the same for you some day, maybe. Nasty bits o' work, them two, I can tell you. Well, thanks a lot, lady. I — '

'Just a minute,' cut in the detective. 'Being of a rather curious temperament — er — Mr. Morgan — I'd very much like to know a little more about your two friends. Just why are they so concerned about your whereabouts? Just what have you been up to, Mr. Morgan? I think I'm entitled to know — after all, haven't I saved your life — according to you?'

A cunningly evil light came into the

little man's rat-like eyes.

'It don't do to talk too much these days, lady,' he said. 'Not even to a smart lady 'tec like you, if you'll let me say so. But I reckon a nod's as good as a wink to a blind man, as the saying goes. You see, I 'ad something those fellows wanted. Not for theirselves did they want it, mind you. No — but for their boss. Them two were only a couple o' stooges, acting for the Big Noise, see? But you don't want to go getting mixed up in a mucky business like this, lady. It's too big and too dangerous — even for a 'tec as famous as you. Sorry if I've given any trouble, lady. If I can ever do anything for you, let me know — the cops'll always tell you where to find Spider Morgan, see?'

It was evident that he did not mean to say any more and Victoria Lincoln was too busy at that moment to question him further out of idle curiosity.

'Well, I suppose you're free to go now, Mr. Morgan,' she said with a shrug of her pretty shoulders. 'The next time you choose a battleground please steer clear of my offices — I might not be quite so successful in aiding you next time. Good afternoon.'

Spider grinned, touched the brim of his greasy cap and slid to the door. He opened it noiselessly, listened intently for a moment and then insinuated himself through the veriest crack of an open door and vanished.

'Well!' said Carol with a slight laugh. 'Quite an exciting morning, eh, Vicky? I wonder just what his little game was?'

'Oh, some inter-gang quarrel, I guess, Carol,' said the detective. 'When thieves fall out — you know. We're not likely to hear any more about Mr. Spider Morgan or his precious pair of friends whose pose as police officers wouldn't have deceived a child. Now bring me the file on the Goodrich case, will you, my dear? I must start serious work some time.'

Miss Lincoln, however, was far from hearing the last of Spider Morgan as she very quickly found out no later than the following morning when she still lay sleeping in her cosy London flat.

The 'phone at her bedside rang and opening her eyes she lifted the receiver languidly and stifled a yawn as she answered.

A moment later she was fully alert, sitting up in bed with a frown creasing her forehead.

'I'll be there as soon as I can, Inspector!' she snapped. 'Within half an hour, anyway.'

She replaced the receiver and hastily dialled another number. A moment later she was speaking to a sleepy-voiced Caroline Gerrard on the other end of the line.

'Meet me at Scotland Yard as soon as you possibly can, Carol,' she said. 'On your way call in at Pamela's home and tell her where we are — then get to the Yard just as quickly as you can. No, I don't know very much — except that there's a serious development in the Spider Morgan affair. Hurry along, child! There's no time to answer questions now!'

Within the hour both Victoria and Carol were seated in Inspector Darrell's office at Scotland Yard and the inspector did not seem to know just how to begin his questioning.

'I — er — I want you to be frank, Miss Lincoln,' he said. 'I want to know exactly what dealings you had with Spider Morgan and I may as well tell you here and now that I know you did have dealings with him. Now when did you last see Spider, Miss Lincoln?'

Victoria did not answer immediately. She was rather nettled at the somewhat cavalier attitude that the inspector was adopting towards her.

'I've nothing at all to hide, Inspector,' she said at last. 'And as far as I am able I will answer any questions you care to put to me — but don't you think it is only fair to tell me why it is necessary to question me at all?'

The inspector looked at her thoughtfully for a moment and then shrugged his shoulders.

'At a quarter to four a.m. today,' he said, 'Spider Morgan was found in the gutter of a Soho back street. The man was unconscious — almost at his last gasp. He had terrible injuries and the doctors fear for his life. He'd undergone as bad a beating-up as I have ever experienced

— and I've seen quite a few in my time. This may be — murder, Miss Lincoln.'

'Good heavens!' said Victoria. 'How ghastly! But — but just where do I come in, Inspector?'

'That's what I want you to tell me,' said the inspector, dryly. 'Spider Morgan consulted you, Miss Lincoln — had some business or other with you. Among the very few things we found in his possession was this — one of your business cards!'

He picked up the card from his desk, allowed Victoria to study it and then dropped it back on to his blotting pad. In a flash Victoria remembered the card she had given to Spider in her office the previous day. Evidently he had stuck it in his pocket for some reason best known to himself.

'This man Morgan didn't consult me, Inspector,' Victoria explained then. 'He more or less forced his way into my office — in search of sanctuary.'

Quickly and concisely then she gave a full account of the whole occurrence and Carol was there to corroborate on every material particular.

21

'He refused to tell me any more than I have told you, Inspector,' she said when her statement was done. 'He did say that the men whom he claimed were following him were what he called 'stooges', working for a 'Big Noise'. So I let him go — and forgot all about the affair until you 'phoned me this morning.'

'H'm!' mused the inspector. 'It may be that these 'stooges' are connected with the attack — but there's no evidence of that at the moment. You've given me a pretty good description of them and I have little doubt that you'd be able to identify them again if you saw them. You said that Morgan claimed to possess something that this 'Big Noise' — whoever he is — wanted. Any idea what that something was — or where Spider had hidden it?'

'He didn't give me any hint at all,' said Victoria shaking her head. 'Just how much do you know about Morgan yourself, Inspector?'

'Oh, quite a packet — though nothing that helps here, however,' replied Darrell. 'Spider's record goes back over a number of years. First convicted of petty larceny about ten years, ago — went 'inside' for eighteen months. Gathered quite a shady reputation in Soho in petty crime; nothing sensational, nothing clever. Twice turned King's Evidence in cases of minor importance, enabling us to obtain convictions of petty gangsters. Been useful once or twice as a stool pigeon or what the popular Press calls 'a copper's nark'. We've always had tabs on him; always been able to pick him up for questioning when we've wanted him. Now it seems that someone has executed a plan of revenge. That would appear to be the only motive for this brutal assault.'

'I wonder what it was that Spider possessed that this 'Big Noise' was prepared to commit murder to obtain?' asked Victoria, more to herself than anyone else.

'Maybe whatever it was, was a stronger motive than revenge?'

'Your guess is as good as mine, Miss Lincoln,' said the inspector and began to gather his notes as a sign that the interview was now ended. 'Well, thanks for your help — at least you have cleared up the point as to how your business card came to be among Spider's personal possessions. I — excuse me . . . '

The 'phone bell at his elbow had buzzed and he picked up the receiver. He listened for a moment and then handed the instrument across the desk to Victoria.

'For you — from your office it seems, Miss Lincoln,' he said as Victoria hastily spoke into the receiver.

'Yes, Pamela! Yes! Oh! Oh! I see. No — don't do anything until I get there. I'll be along with Carol almost immediately.'

Quickly the detective replaced the receiver and rose to her feet.

'Trouble at the office?' queried the inspector, mildly.

'Getting anxious about us — that's all,' said Victoria, evasively. 'Come, Carol, my dear. We must be going. Let me know if there is anything more I can do, Inspector, won't you?'

At the wheel of her own car, whisking up Whitehall en route to her office, Victoria turned to Carol at her side.

'Seems we're going to be closely connected with the Spider Morgan case after all, Carol, my dear,' she said. 'Pamela tells me the office has been ransacked from floor to ceiling!'

'Ransacked?' gasped Carol. 'What on earth for, Vicky — and who would get that way about us?'

'I don't know,' said Victoria slowly. 'But I've a shrewd suspicion that whatever it was that Spider Morgan was beaten up for wasn't found on him by the killers. They then jumped to the conclusion that what they wanted Spider must have hidden in our office somewhere — hence the search. I wonder just what Spider's dangerous secret was?'

2

The secret of the records room

There was no doubt at all that the fire-proof and burglar-proof safe which Victoria Lincoln used as a Records Room was the one spot in her suite of offices that had escaped from as thorough a ransacking as the mind of man could conceive.

Both the outer and inner offices had received expert attention. Every drawer had been dragged open and its contents strewn about the room; every cupboard had been looted and paper, stationery, reference books and the thousand-and-one necessities of a modern office had been piled in an untidy heap. Oilcloth and carpets had been pulled up and in several spots even the floorboards had been prised up and the spaces beneath investigated. Pictures had been removed from the walls and flung aside — and only the Records Room remained intact.

'My goodness! What a mess!' gasped Carol as she and Vicky came in hurriedly straight from Scotland Yard. 'I guess you had a shock when you saw this lot, Pam! Have they been anywhere else in the building?'

'Not that I have heard,' replied Pamela. 'I haven't made any close enquiries, anyway. I was so startled when I opened the door and found the place like this that all I felt able to do was to 'phone Miss Lincoln — and then sit down and stare at the chaos!'

For a minute or two Victoria gazed round at the disorderly scene and then she shrugged her pretty shoulders.

'Straighten things up as quickly as you can, girls,' she said. 'Make a note of anything that you think is missing.'

Then the detective crossed to the door of the steel-clad Records Room and began to examine it closely.

'Whoever broke in here didn't come prepared to tackle a steel-bound safe,' she observed. 'They made a half-hearted attempt to force it — but soon gave it up.

There are fingerprints here, too, Carol. Better take prints of them just as a matter of record. I don't expect them to help much, however.'

Carefully Victoria inserted the key in the lock, threw open the heavy door and from the threshold gazed round the Records Room.

It was in perfect order as far as she could see; no paper and no file out of place. After a moment or two Victoria beckoned Carol to her side.

'While you're helping Pam to straighten up, Carol,' she said, 'I'm going to make a thorough search through the records here — working on the theory that there is something hidden in this room that is so valuable to certain persons that they have risked murder in an attempt to obtain it. Now just what — and where could it be?'

'You think that Spider hid — whatever it was he had — in here while we were screening him from those faked police-officers. Is that it, Vicky?' asked Carol, with a frown.

'Theoretically this strongroom is the only possible place in which Morgan could have disposed of whatever it was that he was carrying,' pointed out the detective. 'That is a fairly safe deduction — made from what we know. Spider told us he was being followed; that was proved when the fake detectives arrived; Spider told us that he had something that a person he referred to as 'the Big Noise' would commit murder to obtain. Spider had no chance to hide anything either in the outer office or my private sanctum. If he's hidden anything somewhere else in this building then there was no need at all for him ever to come into our offices. The only place that he was not under observation the whole time was in this Records Room — therefore it follows that he must have hidden his secret in here.'

'I don't quite see that, Vicky,' objected Carol, thoughtfully. 'Isn't it just as likely that when he left here he took his secret with him? After all — he'd thrown his pursuers off his track — or, at least, you had done that for him — why shouldn't he just carry on from there? Why leave something here? He must have known that he'd have an awful job to recover anything he'd dumped in our strong-room.'

'That's a point, my dear — but it doesn't quite fit in with subsequent happenings,' pointed out Victoria. 'One thing I particularly remember — when the fake officers had gone and Spider came out of the Records Room, I asked him why those two men were so interested in him. His reply was ominous — in the light of what has happened since. He said, '*I had something those fellows wanted*'. Not '*I have something*', note — but '*I had something*'. That, I feel, is significant in itself.

'There are other indications, however. It's obvious that his enemies, whoever they were, quickly traced Spider again after he had left us — for, within twelve hours, his battered body was discovered only a very short distance away from this very spot. Now then — if Spider carried his secret on him when they caught up with him, all they would need to do would be to knock him out and rob him at their leisure. There wouldn't have been any need to beat him up first. No! They caught him; they found that he was not carrying what they were after, so they started in to beat the information out of him. But they went a little too far and Spider Morgan passed out on their hands before they learned what he knew. They realized that their victim might die — and they didn't want a murder rap hung on them — and they knew that he was too knocked about to talk for some time, anyway. Then they did a bit of deducing on their own account. It couldn't have taken them very long to realize that the only place they could think of as being a likely spot for their victim to have hidden what they wanted was my offices! So they came here in a hurry and ransacked the place. Luckily they didn't come prepared to tackle a steel-clad strongroom. Therefore, my dear, if Morgan *did* hide anything on these premises it could only have been in this little room!'

So, while the girls set to work to restore some semblance of order to the ransacked offices, Victoria Lincoln busied herself by conducting a systematic search through the stacks of filing cabinets, card-index drawers and countless cardboard folders.

Just what she was seeking she did not know; a document or papers of some kind, probably. Spider Morgan hadn't been laden with any heavy parcel when he had sought sanctuary; whatever it was that he might have disposed of was something small and compact enough to be carried in a pocket without exciting any undue suspicion.

Pamela and Carol finished tidying the office and then joined Victoria in her search. It was a slow and laborious job, checking through those files and examining scores of letters, papers and cuttings in the hope of discovering a 'stranger' that might be what they sought.

Suddenly Victoria uttered an exclamation, straightened her back and held aloft a small, thin packet wrapped in brown paper and sealed heavily with wax.

'Now we're getting warm!' cried Carol, excitedly. 'Looks as if your theory is correct, Vicky. I've never seen a packet like that in our records before!'

'It's certainly a stranger,' agreed Victoria. 'That, however, doesn't prove that Spider Morgan left it there. But maybe we'll learn a little more now.'

In the privacy of the inner office and with her two assistants watching closely Victoria donned a pair of rubber gloves and then carefully broke the seals of the packet and gently removed the wrappings. Within the brown paper was something further wrapped in a sheet of white notepaper. Discarding this the detective laid bare a gleaming copper plate beautifully engraved with a design that was familiar to all three of them.

'The engraving plate of a five-pound note!' said Carol, with a gasp. 'Don't tell me that little Spider Morgan was a forger! He — '

'*This* was the evidence for which he was attacked!' cut in Victoria.

'With this in his possession, he could have blackmailed the actual forgers to almost any time he liked — or sold his evidence to the police for a fairly substantial reward!'

Victoria set the plate aside for a

moment and turned her attention to the sheet of notepaper. It was thick and of good quality and at its head bore a printed device — a small flag in three embossed colours, and to the right of this the words:

'Aboard the S.Y. *Miranda*

. . . . . . 194 . . . '

'Private notepaper — from a steam yacht named *Miranda*,' said Victoria, quietly. 'I wonder if the copper plate came from there, too! Pamela! Hunt through Lloyd's *Register of Steam and Motor Yachts* will you, please? See if you can find out the owner of the *Miranda*.'

Pamela slipped out to the main office and Victoria very carefully rewrapped the plate and the notepaper in its original wrappings. Then she took another small sheet of brown paper and made a neat parcel, which she proceeded to seal securely.

'If we're right in our deductions, Carol,' she explained, 'then a man has been brutally attacked in an attempt to secure this little packet. It would seem to be a dangerous thing to keep about the place! I think we'll put it in a much safer place than Spider Morgan ever thought of!'

Carefully Victoria Lincoln addressed the package to herself — but the address she gave was neither her home nor her office — it was;

c/o Poste Restante,
G.P.O.,
St. Martin's-le-Grande.
London.

This done she passed the packet to Carol and then took some money from her purse.

'Take this down to Jock at the door, Carol,' she instructed. 'Ask him to get it registered for me — and to hold on to the receipt until I ask for it. Don't leave the building yourself — I've an idea the place is being watched and I don't want you to meet with any trouble!'

Carol slipped down to the entrance hall and handed over the little packet to the commissionaire. When she returned it was to find Vicky studying a page of the yacht register that Pamela had brought into her.

'H'm!' the detective was saying. 'So there are five steam yachts registered here under the name of *Miranda* — and any one of them could be the yacht from which the notepaper came. Well, let's go the routine way to work, girls! We'll send an apparently innocent letter to each *Miranda* owner — hoping for a telltale reply. You can do that Pamela — just say that you've heard that the S.Y. *Miranda* is for sale and ask for particulars. I want you, Carol, to help me fix up a gadget in the Records Room.'

'Then — then you're not going to tell Scotland Yard what happened here last night — and what we've discovered, Vicky?' asked Carol Gerrard, a little uncertainly.

'We have nothing definite to tell them — yet, my dear!' said Victoria, with a smile. 'Let them pursue their own enquiries in their own routine way. For the time being we're working on deductions and theories. After all, none of us could go into a witness box and swear that the packet we found in the Records Room was placed there by Spider Morgan and that it was evidently the motive for his being beaten up. When we have a hide-bound case to offer the Yard, we'll do it, never fear. Meanwhile we'll paddle our own canoe — and maybe learn something really worth while.'

So Carol assisted the detective to fix up a hidden camera behind a ventilating grille inside the Records Room. The silent shutter of this camera would be operated by the opening of the strongroom door — and thus the detective hoped to obtain a photographic record of any person or persons who might break in to continue the search for Spider Morgan's little package.

'You think they will come back again, Vicky?' asked Carol, dubiously. 'After all, they must know now that we'll be on our guard — after what happened here last night. Do you think they'll risk breaking in a second time?'

'They didn't find what they wanted,' pointed out Victoria. 'They know about the strongroom and they will try to discover if Spider left anything inside there. They'll come all right — and tomorrow we'll have a photograph — a photograph that should be very interesting indeed!'

When all these arrangements had been completed it was lunchtime and Victoria went off to keep an appointment with a friend whilst Pamela and Carol adjourned to their favourite restaurant nearby.

In the main hall, Jock, the commissionaire offered Victoria the Post Office receipt for the little packet he had posted for her but the detective asked him to keep it until she asked for it, feeling that it would be quite safe in his custody.

In a nearby pillar box Pamela posted the five letters to the *Miranda* owners and arm-in-arm with Carol crossed the street in search of lunch.

'We're being followed!' said Carol suddenly. 'I thought we were as soon as we came out into Regent Street — now I know, Pam! Look — see that furtive individual just dodging into the doorway there? He's watching us — and not very cleverly either!'

'What do we do, Carol?' whispered Pamela excitedly. 'Lead him up the garden on a wild goose chase?'

'I don't think we need do anything — unless he starts to get funny,' said Carol. 'Just keep a careful eye on him — and get a good description of him to give to Vicky after lunch.'

Though it was clear that the furtive individual was very interested in them he made no move to open up conversation with Carol and Pamela but was just content to sit near them throughout their lunch and stroll at a respectable distance behind them whilst they did a little 'window-shopping' before returning to the office.

Victoria was already at her desk when the two girls returned and quickly they reported their little adventure and gave a detailed description of the man who had shadowed them. Victoria nodded and smiled.

'Somebody is keeping a close watch on all of us,' she said. 'I had a similar experience. I think they're trying to discover by our movements whether we betray any knowledge of Spider Morgan's secret. Keep your eyes open and be on your guard for tricks, girls!'

An hour later another tense situation developed.

There was a knock on the outer office door and a man came quickly to the enquiry counter. Pamela recognized him immediately — it was the furtive individual who had watched her and Carol throughout the lunch hour.

'Could I see Miss Lincoln, please?' he asked, civilly. 'Miss Victoria Lincoln.'

'I'll enquire. What name, please?' replied Pamela, keeping her wits about her.

'My name's Green,' said the stranger. 'But she wouldn't know me. Just tell her I'm a friend of — of Spider Morgan, please!'

Pam controlled her surprise and hastily reported to Victoria in the inner office.

Victoria listened thoughtfully and then nodded.

'Show him in, Pamela,' she said at last. 'And follow the usual routine in the case of emergency. You stand by to take notes, Carol.'

The furtive Mr. Green entered the inner office nervously fumbling with his hat. He refused the chair Victoria indicated and then cleared his throat noisily.

'I — I've come about Spider Morgan, Miss Lincoln,' he began. 'Spider was my friend, see — and — and what's happened to him has rather shook me. I wanted to know if — if Spider left anything with you for me — a little parcel it was, you see. He told me if — if anything happened to him I was to come and see you and ask about the parcel, like. So, if you've got it handy, Miss Lincoln, maybe you'd give it to me right away, like.'

Victoria frowned and then changed her expression to a smile.

'I'm afraid you're talking in riddles, Mr. Green,' she said. 'Your friend Morgan did not come to see me on business — he more or less broke in here with some tale that he was being followed. He certainly did not give me any packet or even a message for you — he never even mentioned your name. Have you been to the police about the matter?'

'The police?' echoed Mr. Green in some alarm. 'Why — why should I go to the police?'

'Only because you seem to know something about Morgan's movements prior to the attack upon him!' said Victoria briskly. 'You say he told you he was coming to see me!'

'Well — he — he didn't exactly say that,' blustered Mr. Green. 'What he said was if anything happened to him I was to enquire about a parcel at the last place he was known to call at, see? He didn't exactly mention your name.'

'And how do you know that mine was the last place Morgan called at before he was attacked?' demanded Victoria sharply. 'The only people other than my office staff who should know that are the police — and the people responsible for his present serious condition! Who told you that Spider came here at all?'

'I — I don't know. I — I just heard it, Miss Lincoln,' said Mr. Green uncomfortably. 'I guess I must have made a mistake. I'm sorry to have troubled you.

Guess I'd better go.'

'I guess you had, too!' said Victoria dryly. 'But don't think I shall forget your visit, Mr. Green. I'm sure the police will be interested to hear about you — and I shall make it my business to tell them of your call.'

'No need to do that, ma'am,' said Mr. Green, backing towards the door. 'I've got nothing to do with Spider — really. Sorry I troubled you. Good afternoon!'

He almost ran from the room and Victoria broke into a light laugh

'Whoever is at the back of all this is very hard up for information, Carol,' she said. 'That was a very crude and bald attempt to find out something about Spider's packet, wasn't it? Either that — or Mr. Green came to have a look round the office to weigh up the chances of breaking into our strongroom. Well, we can afford to keep everyone guessing for a little while. Now I'm going up to the Yard to see if Inspector Darrell's made any headway in solving the Morgan case. You and Pamela needn't wait for me. I'll 'phone you at home tonight if there is any news. Watch your step, however. We have these crooks guessing — and that's almost certain to make them desperate. Goodbye, my dear.'

Victoria found Inspector Darrell in a very harassed frame of mind when she dropped in on him in the late afternoon at Scotland Yard.

'Why do I get all the hardest nuts to crack?' he grumbled. 'Why does an out-and-out little crook like Spider Morgan go and get himself nearly murdered in my area and so give me a job that bristles with headaches? There doesn't seem to be a motive for this attack — no motive at all.'

'I thought you said that it might be revenge,' said Vicky, gently. 'And have you forgotten what I told you? About Spider saying he had something which someone he called 'the Big Noise' wanted?'

'If it was revenge, why have they waited so long for it?' demanded the inspector. 'Spider's not been so active as a 'nark' of recent months; done nothing recently to merit the beating up he got — at least, not as far as we can trace.

And without knowing what the 'something' is that 'the Big Noise' wanted I can't claim that as a motive. There's no two things in this case that tie up together — as far as I can see.'

Victoria was almost tempted to tell him of her own discoveries, but refrained feeling that later on, perhaps, she might have a more complete case to offer him.

'Have you traced Spider's movements before and after he called at my offices, Inspector?' she asked. 'Don't they help at all?'

'I've got witnesses who saw him at definite times between his leaving your Regent Street address and being found in a heap in the gutter of Rose Court, in Soho,' said the inspector. 'According to you, Miss Lincoln, Spider left your office between half-past four and five o'clock. At half-past six he was seen in a Soho café where he was well-known. He was in the company of a seaman, a stranger in town, apparently.'

'A seaman?' echoed Victoria, 'Interesting! Go on, Inspector.'

A seaman and the yacht *Miranda*.

That, to Victoria, was certainly a definite tie-up.

'I've traced the seaman; fellow named Grogan; comes from Southampton,' went on Darrell. 'He gave us a statement — straightforward and easily checked. He had become acquainted with Spider Morgan in Southampton about six weeks ago. Spider had invited him to look him up any time the seaman came to London. It so happened that Grogan chose the night of the attack to do just that. They parted around nine o'clock, however — and Grogan has a cast-iron alibi for his movements from thence onwards. Anyway, Spider was again seen around and in apparently good spirits at about eleven o'clock. Just about that time he had a conversation with a plainclothes C.I.D. man at the corner of Frith Street. Our man vouches for the good spirits; in fact, he states that Spider seemed particularly happy about something and spoke of rosy prospects for his future. After that there's no trace of him at all — until he was found battered unconscious in Rose Court just before four a.m.'

'Queer!' remarked Victoria. 'And what

about his movements *before* he reached my office — in search of sanctuary? Any luck there?'

'Again there's a dead black period,' replied the inspector. 'Morgan's movements are easy to trace up to about two o'clock. He was seen about his usual haunts all the morning. Then, about two o'clock, he seems to have vanished — and the next we hear of him is arriving at your office somewhere about four. Where did he go in those two hours? What was he up to? *You*, Miss Lincoln, say that he said he was being followed. Why? And where from? Who was after him? What had he picked up that was so dangerous — during those two hours in which he was missing from his usual haunts?'

'It's certainly a puzzle,' agreed Victoria. 'Well, if there's anything I can do let me know, won't you? You see, I feel that this is my case almost as much as yours — seeing that my office is involved. Incidentally, how is Morgan? Any chance of an early statement from him?'

'It's doubtful whether he'll live — let alone ever make a statement,' the inspector replied. 'He's out to the wide — and may suffer permanent loss of memory — a condition which will be welcome news to many a crook against whom Spider has given information in the past.'

The Scotland Yard officer paused and then smiled a little superciliously.

'Whilst admitting that you private investigators can use methods which the Yard must regard as unorthodox, young lady,' he said, 'my advice to you in this case is to drop your enquiries. You're a young lady, Miss Lincoln — a smart and pretty one, I grant — but hardly a match for crooks of the calibre that beat men within an ace of death. This is strong meat, dear lady — I'd stay out of it if I were you.'

'You're very gallant, Inspector,' said Victoria, with a mysterious little smile. 'I'll bear your warning in mind. Good-bye.'

★ ★ ★

Victoria spent a quiet evening at home, giving but very little attention to the case except to telephone to Carol Gerrard and learn from her young assistant that the rest of the afternoon had passed normally at the office and they had locked up at the usual time. Both Carol and Pamela had been followed to the bus stop where they had parted to go their separate ways and Carol had been shadowed to her home. Once there, however, her shadower was apparently satisfied; he had withdrawn himself and Carol hadn't seen him since.

Victoria was at her office early the next morning — so early, in fact, that it drew from Jock, the commissionaire, what the detective regarded as a slightly facetious remark.

'What! Back again so soon, Miss Lincoln!' Jock said as the detective entered the lift. 'You are having a busy time, aren't you?'

Victoria smiled and stepped out of the lift on the first floor, fumbling for her keys.

The moment that she opened the outer office door she knew that someone had been there during the night or early morning.

The door of the strongroom stood ajar. She had locked it herself before leaving on the previous afternoon — and neither Carol nor Pamela had a duplicate key.

Passing into her inner office Victoria made a quick search. Nothing seemed to have been disturbed there, however. She removed her hat and coat, once more donned a pair of thin rubber gloves and returned to the strongroom.

The lock did not appear to have been damaged. The tumblers had been turned either by a duplicate key or with the aid of a 'skeleton'.

The records were in a terrible state; every drawer, every file and folder had been ransacked and the contents strewn everywhere. The detective, however, paid little attention to this. She made straight for the ventilating shaft and sighed with satisfaction as she discovered the hidden camera still there and quite intact.

At that moment Carol and Pamela arrived and loud were their expressions of concern when they saw the state of the precious records.

Victoria did not seem at all perturbed, however.

'We'll soon know something about the culprit who did all this, girls,' she said. 'Come on, Carol! Let's develop the negative and get a print.'

In a tiny laboratory and dark room that adjoined her private office, Victoria hastily developed the precious film. Even as the outline of a human figure began to appear upon the film, however, a frown began to deepen on the detective's face.

'Why, look!' cried Carol, suddenly. 'It's the photo of a woman, surely, Vicky! Just where does a woman come into a case like this?'

Victoria said no word as she dried the negative and then set to work to take a print. A few moments later the finished print was on the desk in the inner office and the detective was studying it closely with the aid of a magnifying glass.

'Why, it's you, Vicky,' gasped Carol. 'Whatever went wrong? How does it happen that you've taken a pretty good snap of yourself?'

'It isn't me, my dear!' said Victoria

quietly. 'Though even I thought so myself at first. I thought maybe the selenium cell had gone back on me and the snap had been taken when I opened the door just now. But that isn't so! This is a snap of the person who ransacked the strongroom — and did so rather cleverly made-up to look like me and wearing clothes very similar to those I had on yesterday!'

Carol took the magnifying glass and studied the print closely. While she did so, Victoria buzzed for Pamela and asked her to 'phone down to the hall and enquire if Jock, the commissionaire, could spare a moment or two to come up and see her

'No!' said Carol. 'It isn't you — but it's very like, isn't it? At first glance, anyway. Oh, Vicky! Do you think these people — whoever they are — were clever enough to guess about the camera and did this just to beat you?'

Victoria shook her head.

'I think the intruder dressed up to impersonate me — just to fool Jock and get into the office without arousing any suspicion,' she said. 'Ah! Here is Jock. He'll be able to tell us. Jock — what time was it when you first saw me enter the office this morning?'

'Just on six, Miss Lincoln,' said the commissionaire, promptly. 'The cleaners had only just arrived. Remember? I saw you going up the stairs — the lift hadn't started working. You said you'd come in early for some important papers. The cleaners were just going to do your offices, but you said it didn't matter. I opened the office door for you — with my master-key. Remember now?'

'And — er — about what time did I leave, Jock?' asked the detective, casually.

'Oh, about a matter of an hour later, I suppose,' said the commissionaire. 'Is there — is there anything wrong, Miss Lincoln?'

'Oh no — nothing that matters, Jock,' said Victoria with a smile.

'Just checking up on times, that's all. Thanks very much, Jock!'

The commissionaire withdrew, scratching his head thoughtfully.

'Well, that's that!' said Victoria. 'Quite unwittingly our mastermind, whoever he is, has beaten us, Carol! That disguise was assumed with the intention of fooling Jock and gaining easy admission to the office. It's also fooled me — because I'm no better off now than I was yesterday!'

'That man Green!' said Carol, suddenly. 'He must have come here to study you, Vicky — make a note of the clothes you were wearing — in order to put over this scheme. Well, as you say — that's that! We're no further forward, are we?'

'Nor are the crooks, my dear,' said Victoria, philosophically. 'At least they didn't get what we know they came after. Well, our next hope is the letters to the *Miranda* owners. Perhaps we'll find a definite lead there.'

'I wonder who the woman is who's mixed up in this?' asked Pamela, studying the photograph again.

Victoria shook her head and smiled.

'It isn't a woman, Pam,' she said. 'At least, I don't think it is. The disguise is good enough to fool busy people in the early morning — but look at the hands in that photograph — they're much too big for a woman — note the little finger of the left hand, too. That's a man's signet ring that's worn there. It doesn't matter now, anyway. My scheme has failed, and that's all about it. From now on I don't think we'll have any further ransackings. The crooks must be convinced now that wherever what they want really is — it certainly isn't here! Hullo! Who's this?'

The door had opened; a burly figure stood on the threshold, a figure that Victoria Lincoln wasn't any too pleased to see in all the circumstances.

'Inspector Darrell!' she said. 'What a surprise — so early, too! Any developments, Inspector?'

'Nothing particular,' said the inspector evasively. 'Say, what's been going on here? Looks like a burglary! More work for us!'

'Somebody — disguised as myself and posing as me — gained admittance to the office early this morning and ransacked the place, Inspector,' said Victoria, quickly. 'Do you think it could have anything at all to do with the Morgan case?'

'I don't see the connection,' said the inspector. 'Is there one?'

'Well, Morgan came here for sanctuary,' pointed out Victoria, guilelessly. 'He said he was being followed. I wonder if whoever his enemies were thought, perhaps, that he had hidden something in my office — and so came along to make a search.'

'Could be, I suppose,' said the inspector. 'Do you know if they found anything? Is anything missing that you know of?'

'Can't tell — without a thorough check,' said Vicky and was relieved that the inspector didn't pursue the matter. She didn't want to have to tell him the whole story — yet.

'Oh, well, check up and make a report, Miss Lincoln,' Darrell said. 'I'll send a man down on a routine enquiry later on. What I came to tell you about is this — I think I've found the real motive for the attack on Morgan.'

Victoria looked at him quickly.

'*Have you?*' she said. 'That's just fine. And what is it, Inspector?'

'Robbery!' said the inspector, shortly. 'I've established that Morgan had over a hundred pounds in five-pound notes just before he came to see you, Miss Lincoln. The money wasn't on him when he was found, therefore the attackers must have robbed him. That makes the case take on a less puzzling aspect, doesn't it?'

'I suppose it does,' said Victoria, softly.

She was quite sure that the inspector was utterly wrong — but she did not wish him to discover just yet what grounds she had for thinking so differently and along lines about which Inspector Darrell had not so far dreamed about.

'How did you come by that information, Inspector?' Victoria asked, as casually as she could.

'Rechecking his movements in the morning,' explained the inspector. 'Discovered that he'd paid a call at the Shaftesbury Avenue Post Office. Seems he had a savings account in his own name there. He presented a legitimate withdrawal order for a hundred pounds, properly identified himself and asked for the money to be paid in fivers. I even have the numbers — so they should be traceable. It seems pretty evident that he was beaten up and robbed and that the beating up went a bit too far. Anyway — I'm watching now for any of those fivers to turn up. He didn't say anything to you about money while he was here, I suppose?'

'Not a word as far as I recollect,' said Victoria, and the inspector nodded.

'I just wanted to check on that with you,' he said. 'Well, I'll take myself out of your way while you straighten up. Your unwelcome visitor certainly was busy here, eh?'

Inspector Darrell departed and Victoria looked after him thoughtfully.

The information concerning Spider having been in possession of a hundred pounds on that morning on which he had begged for sanctuary was very intriguing.

'Of course,' she said to Carol a little later, 'Morgan may have had such an amount of money as that on him when he came here — but I rather think he had already rid himself of it; bought something with it — something that he no doubt thought was worth considerably more than what he paid for it.'

'Such as — ?' queried Carol with a frown.

'Such as a copper engraving plate maybe, my dear!' said the detective. 'However — I think we'll tackle the case from the *Miranda* angle. That is a lead that, so far, Inspector Darrell appears to know nothing about.'

3

The owner of the S.Y. Miranda

For the next few days the case of Spider Morgan's violent assault simmered on Scotland Yard's hob, and if Inspector Darrell gleaned any further useful information he confided it neither to the Press nor to Victoria Lincoln.

Spider himself remained in that borderline state halfway between life and death — and was incapable of giving any assistance whatsoever.

Neither did Victoria's offices seem to attract the crooks any further. As a matter of routine the detective sent an official report to the police concerning the illegal entry, but she was forced to add that nothing of value bad been stolen and very little damage had been done. A C.I.D. sergeant arrived to make enquiries; he found fingerprints on the Records Room door, but failed to match them with any in possession of the Yard's Fingerprint Department. He took possession of the photograph that Victoria had obtained of the intruder, but apart from agreeing with the detective that the burglar was probably a man disguised as Victoria herself in order to gain easy entry, the sergeant decided that the photo was of very little value as evidence.

Victoria herself was content to let the matter rest until such a time as she began to receive replies to the letters she had sent to the registered owners of the various yachts named *Miranda* — and before the end of the week these began to produce results.

The first three letters were delivered together and as these produced negative results they helped to narrow down the field. All three stated that their particular yacht *Miranda* was not for sale — and as each letter was written on paper other than similar to the sample Victoria possessed, she was obliged to rule them out of her calculations.

Naturally the detective's interest in the remaining two yacht owners increased —

for she was certain that one or other of them was in some way connected with Spider Morgan and the engraving plate — and so possibly with the assault.

Studying the three letters carefully and with Carol taking notes, Victoria eventually laid them aside and instructed her young assistant to cross the owners' names off their list of 'suspects'.

'In each case the reply has been written on notepaper printed for use aboard the respective yachts, Carol,' Victoria pointed out. 'Neither of them tallies with the sample we found wrapped round the engraving plate. Now let's study the details of the other two *Mirandas.* What does Lloyd say?'

Carol read swiftly from her notes.

''*S.Y. Miranda. Nine-fifty tons. Built H. and W. Ltd.. Belfast, 1936. Registered at Gosport. Owner. Sir W. Barringford-Benton, The Warren, Tamerford, Sussex. Captain, James Herbert, Gosport. Overhauled 1947. Classification A 1'*.

'That's the first one, Victoria. The other *Miranda* is a much smaller vessel. Three hundred tons; built on the Clyde in 1920 and registered at Gourouck. Owner, Neville Court, Esq., Southampton. No captain's name given. Overhauled 1947, and also classified A.1.'

'Good!' said Victoria. 'Now make a note, my dear, to ring up Lloyd's to find out if either or both of those vessels is in commission at the moment and see if you can find out their present position. I — Yes? Come in, Pam!'

A tap had sounded at the office door and Pamela entered quickly.

'A gentleman wishes to see you, Miss Lincoln,' Pamela said, offering a small visiting card. 'A Mr. Neville Court!'

'Neville Court!' echoed Carol. 'Why he's one of the *Miranda* owners we have listed here. Rather strange that he — '

'I'll see him at once!' cut in Victoria, decisively. 'Pam can ring up Lloyd's for that information, Carol. You nip out and bring Mr. Court in here.'

Carol explained to Pamela that she was to ring Lloyd's and make enquiries as to whether the other two yachts named *Miranda* were in commission and a moment later she was confronting a tall well set-up man of prosperous appear-ance.

'Will you come this way, sir?' Carol said. 'Miss Lincoln will see you at once.'

The caller smiled pleasantly and a moment later was seated in Victoria's inner office, his hat and stick on the chair beside him.

'You wrote to me concerning my old tub the *Miranda*, Miss Lincoln,' Mr. Court began. 'I believe you are interested in the proposed sale. Your letter was forwarded to me in town and as I happen to be free this morning I thought I'd look in and give you the necessary particulars. I take it that you are acting as an agent in this matter? You don't propose to buy the old *Miranda* for yourself, do you?'

Victoria fenced for a moment. Her only interest in any yacht was concerned with its connection with an engraving plate and Spider Morgan — but she had no intention of letting Mr. Neville know this.

'At the moment, Mr. Court,' she said quietly, 'my interest in your vessel amounts to little more than idle curiosity.

I wasn't sure that the *Miranda* was for sale.'

'She hasn't been advertised as being on the market,' said Court. 'It's fairly common knowledge, however, that I'm willing to sell her — if I can secure the right price. You know something about steam yachts, I take it, Miss Lincoln?'

'Very little,' admitted Victoria, with a smile. 'So don't be too technical in your description, will you?'

'Look here!' said Court suddenly. 'How about you running down to see the old tub, Miss Lincoln? If you could spare the time I could show you over *Miranda* and you could see exactly what she is like for yourself. That would save a lot of beating about the bush, wouldn't it?'

Victoria was silent and thoughtful for a moment. This was rushing things with a vengeance — and she was more than a little suspicious of Neville Court without the slightest real knowledge of why she should be.

'Where is she lying, Mr. Court?' the detective asked. 'I'm rather busy just now and — '

'She's in dry-dock at Southampton,' cut in Court, quickly. 'Annual overhaul, you know. I'm going down by car this afternoon — I could drive you down if you felt like it. Or you could fly from Northolt, if you wish to save time. I'm sure we'd find it easier to talk business once you'd seen the old *Miranda* for yourself.'

Victoria was intrigued. The very fact that the yacht was lying at Southampton interested her — for Southampton was already a tiny part of the jigsaw puzzle she was trying to fit together. Not so very long ago Spider Morgan had been in Southampton, and he was known to have been in conversation with a seaman from that very port only an hour or so before he was attacked.

'I don't think I can manage this afternoon,' the detective said. 'I might be able to get down tomorrow sometime. Where can I get in touch with you — if I can arrange the trip, Mr. Court?'

'I'm at the Hotel Splendide until about five o'clock this afternoon,' said the caller. 'Then I'll be motoring to Southampton.

The Mariners, Kenton Street, will find me. A wire or a 'phone call and I'll make immediate plans to meet you at the docks.'

'We'll leave it at that, then,' said Victoria. 'I suppose you don't happen to have a photograph of the yacht, do you?'

'No,' said Court, with a smile. 'But I do happen to have a full technical description of her. My skipper made it out for me — in case I decided to advertise. That any good to you?'

'Possibly,' said Vicky reaching forward and taking the folded sheet of paper that the caller took from his wallet and handed over to her.

Immediately Victoria dropped her eyes in order to hide the sudden light of excitement that had sprung into them.

The notepaper was headed in exactly the same manner as had been that which was wrapped round the engraving plate and the detective knew in flash that another valuable clue had fallen into her hands.

She glanced only casually at the written description of the yacht and then she dropped the sheet of paper in her desk.

'I'll communicate with you either late this afternoon or first thing in the morning, Mr. Court,' she said, rising with a smile. 'I trust you have a pleasant trip to Southampton. Good morning!'

Mr. Neville Court rose and reached for his hat and stick. For a moment or two he seemed to hesitate as if about to say something more. He must have changed his mind, however, for a moment later he offered his hand to Victoria; smiled and bowed slightly to Carol and then made for the door. Carol held it open for him and escorted him to the outer office door, pointing to the lift.

When the girl returned to Victoria's side the detective was once more pouring over the sheet of notepaper and Pamela was standing by her side.

'You're quite sure, Pam?' Victoria was saying. 'These are the details Lloyd's gave you — and you're certain they are accurate?'

'As certain as I can be, Miss Lincoln,' said Pamela. 'I took them down as the clerk gave them to me and I read them back as a check. Is there anything wrong, Miss Lincoln?'

'Quite a lot, my dear!' said Victoria. 'If your information is correct then Mr. Neville Court deliberately lied to me! *He* stated very definitely that *his* yacht *Miranda* was in dry-dock at Southampton — yet Lloyd's tell you that the *Miranda,* owned by Mr. Neville Court dropped anchor in Valetta Harbour, Malta, three days ago! Now Lloyds *never* lie — and they very seldom give mistaken information. If *Miranda* is in Valetta — and I feel certain that she is — then just why is Mr. Neville Court so anxious for me to go to Southampton? So anxious that he's willing to drive me down himself?'

'Perhaps — perhaps he is 'the Big Noise' that Spider Morgan referred to, Vicky!' suggested Carol, excitedly. 'Yes! That must be it — it seems as plain as a pikestaff to me now! Spider Morgan by paying a hundred pounds of his own money obtains an engraving plate for forging five-pound notes, a plate that is used by someone called 'the Big Noise'. The Big Noise gets on Spider's track almost at once. Spider seeks sanctuary here and manages to hide the plate and the sheet of notepaper in our Records Room. The Big Noise doesn't realize this at first but gets on Spider's track again, seizes him and beats him up in an effort to get what he wants. Too late he finds Spider has dumped the evidence — and the only place it could be dumped is in these offices. So the Big Noise raids us — twice, the second time because our steel-plated Records Room beat him the first time. He still doesn't find what he's after — and comes to the conclusion that you have hidden the vital evidence somewhere else. Now you are a prominent person in the community, moreover you are a detective with powerful friends and connections at Scotland Yard. The Big Noise can't just kidnap you and beat you up! That would cause too much of a stir — but he plans a more subtle way of getting you into his power — made easier by the fact that you have written to him on the pretext that you have heard his yacht is for sale. So he invites you to go to Southampton — for the sole purpose of finding out from you where that engraving plate now is! All that fits in, doesn't it, Vicky?'

'Fairly sound reasoning, Carol, my dear,' said Victoria, with a smile. 'It does you credit. But you yourself have shown up the weakness in it — if I go to Southampton what else can Court do but kidnap me and try to force the secret out of me? And he'd be no better protected against police enquiries in Southampton than he would be in London. There's another puzzling point, too. You see what Lloyd's say about the other *Miranda* — the one owned by Sir W. Barringford-Benton?'

She pointed to the notes Pamela had given her.

'That vessel is in dry-dock in Southampton!' she said. 'Lloyd's have confirmed the fact. Now what part does she and Sir W. Barringford-Benton play in this little mystery — if any? Carol — I've an idea that I'll have to go to Southampton to find out!'

'Oh, Vicky! Must you?' said Carol, quickly. 'I don't like the set-up a bit! This man is so obviously trying to lure you into a trap. I'm sure he knows you have that evidence against him and he means to get it from you. He's desperate, too — think of what he did to Spider Morgan!'

'I am thinking of what he did to Morgan,' said Victoria, grimly. 'That's one of the reasons why I intend to go to Southampton. Now, Carol! Don't look so agitated, my dear! I'm not going to walk blindly into any trap — I shall take the necessary precautions and make an appointment for Mr. Neville Court to pick me up somewhere. Tell him I have decided to accept his kind offer to drive me to Southampton to look over his yacht. You, Carol, please pay careful attention to my instructions, my dear. You are going to have quite a bit of work to do in the next twenty-four hours or so, I can tell you!'

Still worried and not quite convinced, Carol took her pencil and began to take a verbatim note in shorthand of everything that her friend and employer wished her to do.

A few minutes later Pam announced that she had contacted Mr. Neville Court at the hotel and that he had stated he would be very pleased to pick Victoria up at her office at four o'clock that very afternoon.

Satisfied that the stage was set for the next act of this mystery, Victoria Lincoln rang up Inspector Darrell at Scotland Yard and made a statement to that officer which made him gasp!

★ ★ ★

Mr. Neville Court arrived at Victoria's Regent Street offices promptly at four o'clock to find the detective smartly dressed in tweed coat and skirt and quite ready for the trip to Southampton.

'I'm very glad indeed to have this pleasure, Miss Lincoln,' he said as he took the detective's travelling case. 'I feel so sure you will enjoy the trip, too. My car is at the door. Are you quite ready?'

'Quite!' said Victoria with a smile. 'Goodbye, girls! Don't forget to lock up securely when you leave. I'll be back some time tomorrow or the next day. You know where to find me if you want me — the Mariners Hotel, Southampton. Goodbye.'

From the office window Carol and Pamela watched Victoria handed in to a luxurious limousine and saw the chauffeur-driven car snake into the traffic stream and head west for the Great West Road.

'Well, that's that!' said Carol not without a note of anxiety in her voice. 'I only hope things work out the way she wants them, Pam! I'll never forgive myself if anything serious happens to her. It looks as if she's deliberately asking for trouble.'

'You know Vicky by now, Carol,' said the older Pamela. 'She's at her best in an emergency — and she does hold a card or two up her sleeve. Come on! We'd better get cracking! We've a lot to do, too!'

Meanwhile Victoria Lincoln was sitting back comfortably in the powerful car whilst Mr. Neville Court made light conversation and while his chauffeur skilfully steered towards the suburbs.

For some time Victoria's attention had

been fixed upon the chauffeur. He was a young man, slimly built, clean-shaven and somewhat baby-faced. Victoria noticed that he wore a heavy signet ring on the little finger of his left hand. It rather intrigued her. She couldn't swear to it, of course, but that signet ring looked to be very similar to the one worn by the disguised 'woman' in the photograph that had been automatically taken when the Records Room in the office had been forced.

Yes, the chauffeur could have disguised himself as a woman; might easily have made himself up to look like Victoria herself in order to deceive the commissionaire as had been done. More than ever was the detective convinced that the man at her side was not really concerned about the sale of a steam yacht. She was sure that he had a much deeper motive behind this trip to Southampton — and in all the circumstances that motive could only be concerned with Spider Morgan and the engraving plate.

Once clear of the London traffic, conversation in the car waned a little though Mr. Court did his best to be interesting as they sped along. Victoria answered him politely, but her mind was busy on another task. She had spotted something that at once set her more fully on her guard. She had not expected any action until she had reached Southampton, but it seemed that Mr. Court had other plans.

They had been travelling well over an hour when Victoria turned sharply to her companion and asked a point-blank question.

'Why have we left the main Great West Road, Mr. Court?' she demanded. 'Isn't that the quickest route to Southampton?'

'Matter of opinion, Miss Lincoln,' said the man, easily. 'My chauffeur prefers the Portsmouth Road — less traffic, he seems to think.'

'That would be acceptable — if we were on the Portsmouth Road, sir!' said the detective, sharply. 'At the moment we're travelling on the East Grinstead road — through Sussex. That's rather like going to Liverpool via Bristol! I trust we shan't be too late arriving in

Southampton. I'm a very busy woman, you know!'

Mr. Neville Court was silent for a few moments. His beady eyes had narrowed somewhat though the suave smile was still upon his face.

'I meant to have told you, Miss Lincoln,' he said. 'The circumstance entirely slipped my mind however. I find it necessary to make a call at the home of an old friend of mine. Sir W. Barringford-Benton, of The Warren, Tamerford. You've possibly heard of him?'

Something clicked in Victoria's brain. The name registered immediately. That was the name of the *Miranda* owner whose yacht was in the Southampton dry dock. It looked as if here was another tie-up in the mystery. The detective said nothing about her knowledge of the baronet, however. She managed a disarming smile as she said:

'Well, if you must make social calls, I suppose you must, Mr. Neville. I hope we're not delayed very long, however.'

'That depends on circumstances,' said

the man, with a smile. 'I don't think it will be necessary to detain you very long, Miss Lincoln.'

It was nearly seven o'clock when the car turned off the main road through a pair of wrought-iron gates and on to a well-kept drive.

A few minutes later it stopped at the foot of a flight of stone steps leading up to a mansion that lay well back in its own parklands.

'A drink — or a cup of tea, perhaps?' suggested Mr. Court as he prepared to alight. 'I don't anticipate being much more than half an hour, Miss Lincoln.'

Victoria hesitated but for a second only.

'Thank you,' she said. 'I'd love a cup of tea.'

A butler appeared at the front door as they reached the top of the steps. Neville Court muttered a few words to him as he strode by and into the entrance hall.

'Will you come this way, miss, please,' said the butler and conducted the detective to a beautifully furnished lounge overlooking some spacious lawns.

'You'd like some tea, miss?' the butler

said then. 'I'll bring it almost immediately.'

Victoria stood at the french window and looked at the well-kept lawns.

This home spoke of wealth and opulence — and yet there was something sinister about the place; an air of mystery that seemed to weigh on one heavily.

The silent-footed butler brought a tea tray and vanished again. Vicky poured some tea and was sipping it when Neville Court re-entered the room.

'Now, Miss Lincoln,' he said briskly. 'I think the time has come for you and I to talk serious business, don't you? I don't think you are entirely unaware of the real reason for my bringing you here — or are you?'

'Suppose that you do the talking, Mr. Court,' said Vicky, coldly. 'After all, I am a guest, you know. I hope we don't need to waste much time, I am a busy woman, as I have already told you.'

'I'd be more inclined to class you as a busybody!' said Court harshly. 'You'll burn your fingers if you're not careful, I assure you. What did you do with the packet that Morgan hid in your office? That's what you'll tell me before you leave this house!'

Victoria hadn't expected quite such a blunt approach to this and did not reply immediately.

'Listen, Miss Victoria Lincoln,' continued Court, sneeringly. 'I'll put all my cards on the table and tell you what I know. You seem to be a person of more than average common sense, and I think you'll use that common sense to your own best advantage. Some little time ago a certain article was stolen from on board my yacht *Miranda*. It was stolen by an ex-employee of mine and sold for a hundred pounds by him to that little rat, Spider Morgan. Morgan was trailed from the moment he received the packet until he reached your office. He was trailed again after he left your office and was later picked up and questioned. He did not possess the packet when we found him. We — er — we applied pressure and Spider talked. He told us that he had hidden the packet in your office — but he passed out before he could tell us exactly where!'

'Your statement is tantamount to confessing to a particularly brutal assault, Mr. Neville Court!' said Victoria contemptuously. 'I'm sure the police will be very interested to hear that!'

'We had your office searched,' went on Court. 'The strongroom baffled us for a few hours — and by the time we got in there you had forestalled us and changed the hiding place of the packet. Now, we mean to have that packet back. We know that it is in your possession or in some place where you can easily lay hands upon it — and we know that you have opened that package and are aware of its contents. Now, my dear young lady, I am sure you don't wish for any unfortunate accident to happen to you and I feel sure that you will have sense enough to talk business. Restore that packet to me within the next few hours and I will pay you the sum of two thousand pounds — without any other obligation.'

'In forged five-pound notes, I suppose!' said Victoria, with a contemptuous smile. 'So easy to pay out large sums of money when all you have to do is to switch on a printing press, isn't it, Mr. Court?'

'The money will be paid into your bank — and vouched for as genuine by your own bank-manager, Miss Lincoln,' said Court, urgently. 'Now, what do you say? Is it a deal?'

'No! It most certainly is not!' said Victoria, immediately. 'Even if your offer was a genuine one I would not accept it and so place myself within the reach of the law by compounding a felony. But your offer isn't genuine — so obviously it isn't! Once you know where I have lodged that vital evidence against you, Mr. Court, there is no reason at all why you should not deal with me — in the same manner as you did with Spider Morgan. You see, so long as I keep my secret, I have a reasonable chance of remaining unharmed, Mr. Court.'

Court clenched his fists and took a menacing step forward. Victoria faced him without flinching, however, and he dropped his shoulders and stepped back again.

'There are more ways than one of

making foolish people talk, Miss Lincoln,' he said. 'I've tried the gentlemanly way — now I'll try something less friendly!'

He crossed the room and pressed a bell-push. As he did so Victoria quickly opened her handbag and gripped the deadly little automatic pistol she carried there.

'I think you'd better raise your hands, Mr. Court!' the detective snapped, sharply. 'I don't intend to suffer any brutality either from you or any of your paid thugs. This gun is particularly deadly at short range.'

Court was momentarily surprised. Obediently he raised his hands and stood staring uncertainly at the detective.

Then the gun was suddenly stricken from Victoria's hand. It dropped to the carpet where the butler, coming from behind the detective, suddenly kicked it forward so that Neville Court was able to stoop and secure it.

'So the vixen has teeth?' said Court, sneeringly. 'Your mistake, Miss Lincoln. I have no intention of torturing you — yet. Jackson — kindly bring in the two young ladies that followed us here!'

Victoria's eyes narrowed and a frown appeared on her pretty face.

Court was watching her closely and he knew that once more he held the upper hand.

'You're surprised, Miss Lincoln?' he said. 'You shouldn't be, you know. I felt very certain that you wouldn't walk into my trap without taking some precautions for your own safety. You had your two assistants follow us from London in your own car, didn't you? I rather guessed that would happen — and had them tailed for safety's sake. The moment we arrived here I issued instructions for your friends to be intercepted and detained. Ah! Here they are now!'

The door opened and to Victoria's concern she saw Carol Gerrard and Pam Wentworth urged forward by the burly silent-footed butler.

'Now the party is complete, isn't it, Miss Lincoln?' said Neville Court with a satisfied smirk. 'Listen, girls! I have just been explaining to Miss Lincoln that I am prepared to go to considerable lengths to regain possession of a certain package that was stolen from me. Miss Lincoln, whilst admitting that she knows where that package is definitely refuses to part with the information. I feel sure that her refusal was caused partly by her confidence that you were following close behind her and would be able to give assistance in the event of trouble. I feel sure you are convinced now, Miss Lincoln, that no help will be forthcoming from your young assistants!'

It certainly was a bitter pill, but Victoria had no intention of letting Court see this.

'Well, you seem to have us all nicely in your clutches, Court,' she said. 'Just what do you propose to do now?'

'I'm going to call Jackson in, Miss Lincoln!' snapped Court viciously. 'It was Jackson who dealt with Spider Morgan. Pity you didn't see Morgan when he was found — you'd realize then how thorough he is. Ah, Jackson! Miss Lincoln isn't inclined to string along with us in quite the way we require. I want you to take one of these girls and show Miss Lincoln just how you set to work to make close-mouthed people talk. Start on the fair-haired one — Carol, isn't it?'

Jackson cat-footed forward and Carol shrank back as the butler reached to seize her.

'Stop!' snapped Victoria suddenly. 'You win, Court! Leave my staff alone — I'll tell you what you want to know!'

'I thought you'd see sense, dear lady!' said Court with a malicious grin. 'Well? Where's the packet?'

'Before I tell you that I must have some guarantee of their safety,' said Victoria, quietly.

'You have my word that no harm shall come to them — or you — once I have the required information,' said Court, quickly.

'I'm afraid your word is not good enough, Mr. Court,' said Vicky coldly. 'Would it be possible to see your so-called friend, Sir W. Barringford-Benton? This is his home — so you told me.'

'That's not possible — just now,' said Court, hurriedly. 'Sir Walter is — well, he is not available.'

'I didn't think he would be!' said

Victoria with a rather puzzling smile. 'It doesn't matter, anyway. This is what I suggest, Mr. Court. Allow my two assistants to leave at once and return to their homes and families. When they have reached their homes I want them to ring me up here and assure me of their safety. Once I have that assurance I give you my word I will tell you where the package is and just how you may obtain it.'

'No! The moment I let them go they'll rush straight to the police!' snapped Court. 'Nothing doing!'

'But I will put both girls under a solemn vow of silence,' persisted Victoria. 'They will promise me not to take any further action at all unless I give them permission. You have to take a chance — after all, you'll still have me in your power, Mr. Court!'

Neville Court paced the floor in earnest thought for a few moments. Then he came to a sudden decision.

'I'll take the chance!' he snapped. 'But Heaven help you — and them if they double-cross me. You hear that, girls?'

Neither Carol nor Pamela paid any

attention to him. Victoria, however, made them give her a solemn promise that they would go straight home and say nothing to a soul about what had occurred. Reluctantly they gave the promise — and Victoria knew that it could be relied upon.

It was nearly eight o'clock when Carol and Pam left the rambling old house. Before half-past nine they had both 'phoned to Victoria — having been given the number — and assured her of their safety.

When the detective replaced the receiver for the second time she turned to the waiting Neville Court with a quiet smile.

'Now, Mr. Court,' she said, 'We can continue our discussion. The girls are safe and I'm ready to carry out my part of the bargain.'

'Where is the package?' snapped Court. 'How soon can I get hold of it?'

'At this precise moment,' said Victoria calmly glancing at her wristwatch, 'the copper engraving-plate from which you forged five-pound notes and which I found wrapped in a sheet of notepaper bearing the name of your yacht *Miranda*, is in the hands of Detective-Inspector Darrell at Scotland Yard. Just how you propose to get it back from him is a matter for you yourself to decide, Mr. Court!'

4

Inspector Darrell makes a move

Just before she had left her office in the company of Mr. Neville Court, Victoria Lincoln had had a conversation with Inspector Darrell at the Yard — a conversation that had left the police officer gasping.

Yet all she had actually told him was that she thought she had a clue in the Spider Morgan assault and battery case; that she was going to follow it up and make sure of its value before telling him about it and that there might be some danger to herself in the process.

She had then told him that she would telephone him that evening before eight o'clock, probably from Southampton and she warned him that if that call failed to come through from her then it would indicate that she was in as grave a danger as Spider Morgan had been.

90

In that event the inspector was asked to proceed at once to St. Martin's-le-Grande and there pick up a registered parcel addressed to Victoria Lincoln at the Poste Restante, open and examine it and proceed to take such action as he thought might be necessary.

'And work quickly, Inspector!'

Victoria had finally said. 'When you see what's inside that parcel if you have to get it — you'll realize that I stand a very good chance of being beaten-up as badly as was Spider Morgan. Goodbye!'

Of course, by eight o'clock, no call had come through from Victoria. By ten past eight the inspector was at the G.P.O. making his preliminary enquiries.

The parcel was duly found; a certain amount of red tape had to be cut before the inspector was allowed finally to open it — and when he discovered the engraving plate and the clue of the letterhead he returned to Scotland Yard and began to mobilise all the forces at his command and set them to work.

Contact with another department at the Yard revealed that officers had been for sometime investigating the mass forging of a large number of five-pound notes most of which circulated abroad. Samples of these taken from the Yard dossiers proved that one at least had come from the engraving plate now in their possession. The clue of the headed notepaper was the obvious lead to follow and by routine methods similar to those used by Victoria Lincoln but not nearly so swift in producing results, Inspector Darrell isolated the two *Mirandas* owned by Mr. Neville Court and Sir W. Barringford-Benton respectively and officers were put on to follow up these clues as far as they would lead.

The inspector did not forget that Victoria Lincoln had a secretary and a young assistant but he had no knowledge of their home addresses and could do no more than put a man on to the task of tracing them and seeking information from them as soon as possible.

Before midnight the inspector's plans were well under way and soon after, results began to come in. Satisfied that he had done everything that was immediately possible Inspector Darrell rang for a police car and set off for a destination that only he and his driver knew.

Meanwhile Victoria Lincoln was still a prisoner in the gloomy old house in Sussex where Neville Court had taken her. Court's rage when the detective calmly announced the whereabouts of the coveted packet was so great that it was only by an effort that he withheld from striking her.

'You — you double-crossing liar!' he snarled. 'Where's the packet! I'll have it — even if I have to — '

'Kill me for it?' suggested Victoria calmly. 'Make yourself a murderer, Mr. Court? Am I worth it? It's your own fault that you find yourself in this position. Had you taken me straight to Southampton I would have 'phoned the inspector — and the packet would not have reached his hands — yet.'

'You — you — ' spluttered Court but words failed him in his rage and be pushed the bell and held his finger on it until Jackson, the butler, appeared.

'The jig's up!' he snarled when the butler appeared. 'The police have the plate — no doubt on our track right now. Get the boys together. We're leaving for Southampton right away. 'Phone Jimmy Herbert — Gosport 81. Tell him to get the *Miranda* out of dry dock and have her standing by with steam up — it's our one chance of getting away. Move, man — move! Don't stand dithering there!'

'And the woman?' asked the butler grimly. 'What happens to her?'

'She goes with us!' snapped Court. 'Might find use for her as a hostage — if not — well, a nice quiet burial at sea, I think! Take her along with you now!'

The butler advanced slowly and determinedly.

'Keep your hands off me, you brute!' snapped Victoria, her eyes blazing.

Jackson set his lips grimly and continued to advance. His great arms came out to encircle the detective. Victoria suddenly swerved sideways, gripped one of the outstretched arms in a quick movement, pulled forward and jerked back again almost in one movement — a ju-jitsu trick she had mastered long ago.

The butler lost his balance, went staggering forward and crashed headlong into the wall. Dazed and bewildered he dropped to his knees and Court uttered an oath and then pulled a gun and faced the determined Victoria.

'You're going with us — alive or dead!' he snarled. 'Now get moving or I'll kill you right here and now!'

Victoria realized that she was fighting overwhelming odds. In his present state of mind Neville Court was certainly likely to shoot her down in cold blood. Discretion always was the better part of valour — never more so than in a case like this.

She allowed Court to shepherd her from the room. In the dining room beyond, others of the gang were gathered and quickly the detective was seized, her arms bound behind her and a gag thrust in her mouth.

'Now get moving — all of you! Get the limousine, Brett,' Court snapped. 'We have to be in Southampton before dawn. The jig's up — if we don't get out now we're all done for! Get it?'

By midnight the powerful limousine was well on the way to the coast. Brett, the baby-faced chauffeur was at the wheel, Court beside him. In the rear seats Victoria was sandwiched between the burly Jackson and the man who had once called at her office giving the name of Green. Opposite sat two other figures the detective knew she had seen before — the two men who had posed as police officers when they had come to the office hot on the trail of Spider Morgan.

Dawn was just breaking as the car sped into the north side of Southampton and down through Bargate to the docks.

At the main gate Court ordered the chauffeur to pull up and then leaned through the window and signalled the constable on duty there.

'I'm Sir W. Barringford-Benton, my man,' he said officiously. 'My yacht *Miranda* was ordered out of dry-dock early on and should be standing by with steam up at one of the quays. Know anything about her?'

'*Miranda*, sir? Yes, that's right. Cap'n Herbert went aboard couple of hours ago, sir,' the policemen replied. 'Quay Twenty-four, sir — right ahead.'

He stepped back and opened the dock gates and allowed the car to enter. He watched it wending its way to the waterfront and then grinned slyly as he made his way into the police-room beside the gate and picked up a telephone receiver.

'Party for the *Miranda* just arrived, sir,' he reported to someone over the wire — 'six men and a lady. Very good, sir! I'll be on watch.'

The limousine picked its way through the dockside in the growing light and turned along the side of Quay 24.

There was the smart and graceful steam yacht, close to the side, steam hissing from her winches, smoke rising lazily from her yellow-painted stack and her gangways down.

'Get aboard!' snapped Court over his shoulder. 'Take the girl with you, Toby — you give a hand, Sam. Brett, you see about getting the car on board — we may be glad of her on the other side. All right — up the gangway, all of you!'

Court did not seem to notice how quiet it all was on deck. He ran lightly up the gangway and waited at the top for the two men to bring Victoria Lincoln up with them.

'Follow me — into Number One stateroom!' Court snapped over his shoulder and then stepped briskly along the shining white deck towards a mahogany door set amidships.

He thrust open the door and strode in boldly. The two men behind him urged Victoria forward. Her hands were still bound behind her back and the gag was still in place.

'All right, Toby — leave her here,' Court growled. 'Then get aft and tell the skipper I want him, I — what the — Who the hell are you? What're you doing here?'

For the first time Neville Court had glimpsed the burly figure standing in the shadows at the far side of the stateroom. That burly figure now moved slowly and somewhat ponderously forward — to reveal the fact that two other men stood behind him.

Neville Court uttered an oath and

backed towards the stateroom door — but even as he did so it swung open and another man stepped inside and hastily pinioned his arms behind his back.

The burly man said no word but hastily removed the gag from Victoria's mouth and then sought for a knife to cut her bonds.

'Seems like my call here is rather opportune, Miss Lincoln,' the burly man said at last. 'Are these the — the *gentlemen* from whom you rather expected a beating-up?'

'Correct, Inspector!' said Victoria with a great gasp of relief. 'And am I glad to see you! Apparently you learned a lot from that little package I told you to pick up!'

'Quite a lot — but there are still several gaps that require filling,' said Inspector Darrell. 'Supposing you do a little introducing, Miss Lincoln!'

'This man has two identities, apparently, Inspector,' said Victoria pointing to Neville Court. 'When I first met him he called himself Court — Neville Court but I have reason to believe that he is also Sir

W. Barringford-Benton.'

'The owner of this yacht? Interesting!' said the inspector. 'Go on, please!'

'These other two are members of the gang,' said Victoria,' and if you need an immediate charge against them I can lay it — they recently presented themselves at my office posing as police officers. There's the chauffeur Brett, too. He's outside on deck somewhere. I'm pretty certain he burgled my office — disguised as me! I can't claim that Court kidnapped me — because I accompanied him of my own free will — but I can charge him with offering me a bribe in an attempt to defeat the ends of justice and also with threats against the persons of my two assistants, Carol and Pamela. Will that be enough to go on with?'

'Just what is all this?' blustered Court angrily. 'What right have you aboard my yacht, Inspector? What charge do you make? How dare you — '

'In the first place I have a properly issued search warrant, Mr. Whatever-your-real-name-is,' said Inspector Darrell. 'A warrant authorising me to search the

Miranda in an attempt to locate a hidden printing press — a printing press that had been extraordinarily busy turning out forged banknotes.'

'And having made your search and found nothing you have no further right on board!' snapped Court. 'I'll make you sit up for this! I'm — '

'You'll get a chance to say your piece in due course, my friend,' interrupted the inspector. 'Meanwhile let me warn you — officially. You now know me to be a police officer. I hold a warrant for your arrest on the charge of attempted murder of one William Morgan, known as 'Spider' Morgan and I must warn you that anything you say will be taken down and maybe used in evidence. O.K. Sergeant — take him along. Pick up the others, Herrick — they're charged as accessories.'

Cursing and struggling Neville Court was borne away and Victoria Lincoln found herself alone in the stateroom with her rescuer.

'Congratulations, Inspector!' Victoria said with a smile. 'You must have put in a

101

hard night's work to get here in the nick of time. But can you pin anything that will stick on to Court or whatever his name is? Did you find a printing press aboard his yacht?'

'Not *this* one,' admitted the inspector. 'But then this isn't the only *Miranda* registered at Lloyd's. There is a smaller craft registered in the name of Mr. Neville Court — a mere three-hundred ton affair. Well secreted in her after hold she has a modern electric printing press on which there is no doubt that a large number of forged notes have been turned out.'

'But that *Miranda* is in Malta — Valetta Harbour,' said Victoria. 'Has been for the last three or four days. Ah! I see! You must have discovered that within an hour of opening the little parcel I told you about last night, Inspector. In all there were five *Mirandas* listed in Lloyd's, weren't there? I take it that you had each one traced and search warrants issued against all of them.'

'Right!' agreed the inspector. 'Thanks to your tip I learned that two of them are out of commission, laid up; one in the Mersey, another in Fowey. A third was in commission and was located off Burnham. It was easy to check up and get negative results from all of those three. There remained this *Miranda* — and the one in Malta. I decided to search this one myself because you mentioned Southampton in your last message to me. The other was covered by our overseas department. It was raided in Valetta Harbour soon after midnight last night — and the printing press and several hundred thousand pounds in forged notes discovered. The entire crew was arrested and — well, here we are!'

'Really good work, Inspector!' said Victoria with a smile. 'I congratulate you.'

'I have to admit that without your help I might have been weeks on the case, Miss Lincoln,' acknowledged the Yard man. 'But all that doesn't let you out, young lady! I've a mind to make serious trouble for you — suppressing important information in a serious case, indeed! What have you to say to that?'

'Me! Suppressing information, Inspector?' said Victoria, looking innocent. 'Come, come! You mustn't make serious allegations like that.'

'Listen! A man came into your office and hid an important packet for which he was subsequently half-murdered,' said the inspector, 'You found that packet and instead of turning it over to me — or to the Yard you — '

'But I *did* turn it over to you, Inspector!' Victoria pointed out. 'With the result that you've made several important arrests.'

'H'm!' said Darrell. 'But there was a delay in turning in the evidence — a delay of several days, during which time — '

'During which time I unearthed further evidence which should make your case complete,' cut in Victoria. 'For instance, I've told you that Neville Court and Sir W. Barringford-Benton are one and the same man. That should help you to prove several things — that Court was able to fake alibis, for one thing. I can also give evidence that Court confessed to organizing Spider's assault — he even told me that it was the butler, Jackson, who did the actual beating-up. Doesn't that help?'

'I must admit that it does,' said the inspector with twinkling eyes. 'But tell me this, Miss Lincoln — did you know that the Treasury has recently offered a very large reward indeed for information leading to the uncovering of this forged currency gang?'

'Well, now — that's rather a leading question, Inspector!' said Victoria with a little smile. 'I hope I do not *have* to answer that!'

'Good enough, young lady,' said Darrell, still smiling. 'A nod's as good as a wink. I always knew you were pretty smart. Heigh-ho! I guess I can do with some sleep.'

'Me, too,' said Victoria. 'But I must telephone to Carol first — she and Pam will be worried stiff until they hear from me!'

* * *

A few days later Scotland Yard released the news of the round-up of the currency

105

forgers and the capture of Spider Morgan's attacker and added the information that Spider had recovered consciousness — but that his memory was seriously impaired and he could remember nothing of what had happened to him before or after his vicious beating up. The newspaper story, however, was not entirely complete in its details — it made no mention at all of the part played in the case by Victoria Lincoln and her two young assistants.

'Which is all to the good, Carol,' said Victoria in her office when she had read the newspaper reports. 'That sort of publicity only puts the underworld wise to us — and that would hamper us in future cases. Spider's loss of memory may be just a ruse on his part — an attempt to evade awkward questions from the police or his fellow crooks. However, that doesn't concern us.'

'One thing puzzles me greatly, Vicky,' said Carol thoughtfully. 'How did you know that Neville Court and Sir W. Barringford-Benton were one and the same man?'

'Pure deduction, my dear,' said Victoria. 'Aided by what is sometimes called a woman's intuition. I knew that Sir W. Barringford-Benton lived in a house called The Warren, in Sussex. I knew that he owned a yacht called *Miranda*. When I found that Neville Court was taking me to The Warren I asked myself just what connection he had with the baronet. When we reached the house and Court walked into it as if he owned it — well, I deduced that he *did* own it — and I was right. It was a shrewd move on his part. He could play the Society baronet on the one side — and the polished gentleman-crook on the other — and use both his identities to further his forgery racket when he needed to. But like all crooks he eventually made the mistake that led to his undoing. If he'd been more careful with his treatment of Spider Morgan — well, we might never have heard of the S.Y. *Miranda* and that printing press.'

'And we certainly shouldn't have received that very nice and *very* substantial Treasury reward!' said Carol. 'That certainly was a nice gold frame into which to put the *Miranda* case, wasn't it?'

With the smile that was so characteristic of her Victoria Lincoln agreed.

2

IN LUCKY HORSESHOES, EVEN

Amongst her countless loyal friends and admirers Miss Lincoln held none in higher esteem than Mr. Desmond Carter, editor of the famous London daily newspaper, *Express and Star*. So when one afternoon, Caroline Gerrard handed her the 'phone with the news that, 'A Mr. Carter wants you, Miss Lincoln,' she took it with a happy smile of anticipation.

Carol busied herself at her desk till her employer had finished talking. Then:

'Is it a case for us, Vicky?' she asked.

'It is indeed, my dear! There's been a bank robbery at Redhill, near Reigate — a man's been found dead, too; they think it's murder! Mr. Carter wants us to go over right away and hear the story.'

Carol's nerves tingled anew with that supreme thrill of the chase as she went for her hat and coat.

That was the best part of this job, she told herself, as she waited for her boss to get ready. You never knew what adventure the day might bring . . .

Mr. Desmond Carter was something over forty — bluff, efficient, refreshingly sincere. Victoria and Carol were shown immediately into his office.

'Ah, I'm very pleased to see you again, Miss Lincoln!' Mr. Carter said, breezily. 'And this is the assistant you were telling me about — Miss Gerrard?'

'That's right,' Victoria murmured. 'Carol, my dear, meet London's leading journalist. He comes first on our list of folks we must be very nice to!'

Caroline and Mr. Carter were laughing as they shook hands. Then the famous editor waved them into chairs beside his desk.

'And now, Miss Lincoln — to business. I believe you've done quite a bit of Bank of England work, haven't you?'

Victoria Lincoln replied that she'd had that honour. Mr. Carter went on: 'Very well — I think you may be able to help us to get a first-rate story from this affair. It has some extraordinary features which I think can best be investigated by a private detective . . . and especially, I think, by two young ladies of such proved capabilities as your good selves!'

He bowed slightly to Victoria and Carol. Miss Lincoln smiled.

'Really, Mr. Carter — if I wasn't so thick-skinned you'd have me blushing!'

'Ah, well spoken, my dear! Anyway, here are the facts as we have them. The bank in question is the National Farmers', which stands at the corner of Redhill High Street and Nayland Avenue. The bank carries very heavy deposits — amongst its customers are over half a dozen big factories in the Reigate area.

'The manager is a James Reynolds. His office is immediately above the bank's steel-and-concrete strongroom — into which, every Thursday, a huge sum of cash is placed in readiness for the various factory cashier's withdrawals on Fridays; to pay their workers' wages. The door of this strongroom can be seen from the street, and at night there's an electric light above it, shining directly on it — so that the policeman on his beat can look in as he passes to see that everything is in order.

'Also, there was a night watchman employed there — an Army pensioner named Frederick Palmer. Every half-hour the policeman passed on his beat — and the arrangement was that he should look into the bank and await Palmer's signal that all was in order before he proceeded.

'We come to last night.' Mr. Carter glanced at his notes:

'Police-constable Bruce Wetherall stopped as usual before the bank and looked through the window towards the strongroom door. To his surprise he saw that the light above it was out. He waited for a few moments, but all was quiet — and there was no sign of Palmer. He became alarmed, went round to the side door of the bank. To his amazement, this was standing ajar. He pushed it open, went in, called Palmer by name; but there was no answer.

'Wetherall says he noticed a sickly, sweet smell strong on the air. He thought he recognized it as chloroform.

'He went through the general office,

114

which was empty. In Reynolds' office the light was on — and here he found Frederick Palmer. He was tied hand and foot with leather straps, and there was a pad fastened round his nose and mouth. Here Wetherall found the explanation of the sickly odour; for above Palmer's head was a tin can hanging from the picture rail — with holes in its bottom through which liquid dripped on to the pad covering Palmer's face.

'Wetherall snatched off the pad, tried to revive Palmer — but he was too late. The watchman was dead. Wetherall then 'phoned for the ambulance. The surgeon found several scratches on Palmer's left hand — recently made, too; smears of blood were still round them.

'Leaving another policeman to guard the bank, Wetherall went to arouse the manager, who lived a little way down on Nayland Avenue. This was at three-thirty in the morning, remember — but there were lights showing in Reynolds' house. When Wetherall knocked, Reynolds answered the door himself. He was dressed to go out, and in the hall Wetherall saw a large attaché-case and a travelling rug!

'Reynolds' face paled as he heard Wetherall's story. 'This is going to look bad for me, constable,' he said. 'Fact is, I was just going away on a holiday. I left a note at the bank explaining everything to the directors.'

'Wetherall says he didn't believe this story; it was rather feeble, as I think you'll admit, Miss Lincoln. So Wetherall took Reynolds back to the bank. There, Reynolds went to his desk, searched in vain for his keys and the note that he said he'd left there. There was no sign of them; and when they checked up the cash in the strongroom they found nearly fifty thousand pounds was missing!'

'So I suppose James Reynolds is now under arrest?' Victoria asked.

'He certainly is. He's charged with robbery and with causing the death of Frederick Palmer.'

'I see. Is there anything known about him?'

Desmond Carter nodded.

'There is. He's an ex-convict. Some-how, he managed to get a clerk's job at

116

the bank about ten years ago . . . and he's worked himself up to be manager.'

'A pity he's strayed from the straight and narrow path again after all those years!' Miss Lincoln murmured. 'What's your personal opinion, Mr. Carter? Do you think he's guilty?'

'W-ell — it's hard to say. The only thing that gives me a faint doubt is this: Reynolds insists on saying he's innocent. Surely a guilty man, faced with such evidence against him, would know he stood no chance, and would confess? Yet the bank president has written me — saying he is convinced of Reynolds' innocence.'

'I suppose Reynolds gives some explanation for his running away suddenly like that?'

'Yes — and it's a very thin story, too. He says he'd been recognised by a man who served in Dartmoor with him — he'd received a letter demanding money . . . or else this man threatened to tell the bank officials of his record as a convict. So, rather than be blackmailed for the rest of his life, Reynolds thought the best thing he could do was to clear out and start afresh in another part of the country. He says that's why he left the note and his keys, and was all ready to depart when Wetherall came to the house.'

'And you think it's all lies?'

'Well . . . neither letter nor keys were found. What d'you think?'

Miss Lincoln glanced at Carol, as she usually did when she wanted her to take particular notice. Carol nodded slightly, leaned forward in her chair.

Victoria said:

'Look at it this way, Mr. Carter. Suppose Reynolds *did* do it? Suppose he *did* take the money and left everything so that it looked as if a crook had broken into the bank, forced his way into the strongroom? And suppose he *has* made up the story about the blackmailing letter just to give himself an excuse for running away with his loot? Surely he'd have left that letter and keys in his desk to support his story, wouldn't he?'

She turned to Caroline.

'Carol, my dear, I want you to follow carefully. D'you see what I'm getting at?'

'Yes, Miss Lincoln!' Caroline answered eagerly. 'You mean the very fact that the letter and keys are missing means that someone actually did break into the bank, killed Palmer, took the money — and the keys and letter, so that everyone would think Reynolds was the thief!'

'Exactly.' Victoria nodded encouragingly. 'How about you, Mr. Carter?'

'I agree. That's just what I meant when I said I wasn't satisfied with the case. There's lots of points which don't seem to fit. So will you have a shot at it for us, Miss Lincoln? Make a few discreet enquiries, and so on; I think you know pretty well what I want . . . a really good, thrilling story — the more sensational, the better I'll like it! And we want to see the guilty party brought to justice!'

Victoria nodded thoughtfully.

'Very well, Mr. Carter. You know — I'm rather puzzled by those scratches on Palmer's left hand. Were they very deep?'

'I see your point, Miss Lincoln . . . no, they weren't deep enough to suggest a struggle. There were some on the right hand, too, though not so many.'

'H'mm. Would it be possible to see Mr. Reynolds?'

'By all means. I'll write you an order immediately,' said Mr. Carter.

* * *

Rain was falling fitfully as Miss Lincoln and her assistant stepped through the dark gateway of Brixton Prison. A warder led them to Reynolds' cell, where the distracted ex-manager sat gazing vacantly before him.

Victoria explained their business.

'You're going to help me?' Reynolds asked, his pale eyes brightening. 'You believe I'm innocent?'

'I didn't say that, Mr. Reynolds. Nevertheless, we're making enquiries on your behalf. We're going down to Redhill — so if there's anything you can tell us that you think will help . . . '

He looked up eagerly. Carol thought he was quite good-looking, with his sensitive face and dark wavy hair. It was hard to imagine him a bank robber. Harder still to think of him as a murderer . . .

He said:

'Will you see Mabel for me, Miss Lincoln? Mabel Palmer . . . she's Fred's — the night watchman's — daughter . . . we were — Well, walking out together . . . we planned to be married. This terrible affair will — well, I don't know what she'll think! They wouldn't let me see her. They — '

Miss Lincoln nudged her youthful assistant.

'This is very interesting, Mr. Reynolds! They didn't even tell me Palmer had a daughter!'

'Yes . . . she's very beautiful. We kept our friendship rather a secret, because of her dad working at the bank. You'll see her, though, Miss Lincoln? Tell her I'm innocent — that I'd rather have died than have anything like this happen. They can't hang me — they can't send me to prison for something I never did, can they?' He covered his eyes with his hands, bowed his head.

Victoria Lincoln spoke softly.

'Don't worry too much, Mr. Reynolds! If you're innocent, everything will turn

121

out all right. We'll certainly see Miss Palmer and convey your message. What's her address?'

'Four, Nayland Avenue — just across the street from the bank's side entrance. Ah, she's the sweetest girl in the world! And lots of men in Redhill think so, besides me! Even Constable Wetherall, who arrested me — he's asked her to become engaged to him, more than once!'

Carol felt a sudden tingle of excitement shoot through her as Miss Lincoln gripped her arm.

'Ah — so you had a rival, eh, Mr. Reynolds?'

'Yes, miss. He used to write her fancy love letters, bits of poetry, and so on. Mabel showed them all to me — we had many a laugh together over them.'

'Very interesting, I'm sure! Now, Mr. Reynolds — did you tell Mabel about that letter you received . . . I mean that one from the man who said he'd known you in — er' — Miss Lincoln coughed — 'in Dartmoor?'

'Yes, I told her. It was largely on her advice I decided to clear out. I decided to go up north — to Newcastle, in fact, where I have some good friends . . . and she was going to join me in a week or so.'

'I see. Have you any theory as to what happened? I mean, about the bank door being open when Wetherall passed on his beat?'

Reynolds shook his head in bewilderment.

'It's an absolute mystery, Miss Lincoln. It's hard to believe — but all I can think of is, that Fred Palmer must have slipped out for a second, perhaps across to his house, and left the door open. The thief got in then — and when Palmer returned, knocked him unconscious and made sure he stayed unconscious by fixing the tin of chloroform above his head. I've thought so much about the whole extraordinary affair that my head's fairly buzzing, miss!'

They left shortly after. They entered the car and Victoria Lincoln drove slowly out of London on the Reigate road. It was twenty to five when they reached the outskirts of the sleepy little town of Redhill.

They found the National Farmers' Bank without any difficulty — a two-storied, squat, red-brick building in a prominent position in the High Street. Victoria parked the car round the corner, in Nayland Avenue — almost opposite the side door of the bank.

They left the car and went over. Through a window they could see the large general office, with the strongroom door in the background. Two clerks were busy stowing away their ledgers. Their day's work was nearly over . . .

'This will be the door that Wetherall found open,' said Caroline, as they walked past. 'Where's the first stop, Miss Lincoln? Number Four?'

The detective nodded. Nayland Avenue was a thoroughfare of pretty villas, semi-detached — each block an exact replica of its neighbour. Palmer's house was just across the road and maybe twenty yards up.

As they walked up the garden path the pink curtains covering the front windows parted slightly.

'Someone's seen us!' murmured Carol.

The slight movement caused Miss Lincoln to glance towards the window; a box of black tulips decorated the sill and Miss Lincoln, a lover of flowers at any time and especially interested in this rare variety, stepped over the small lawn to get a closer look.

The sill was covered with thin dirt that had trickled from the box; so that it was easy to see where something shaped like a half-moon had lain very recently. Victoria traced the faint mark with her finger.

'Looks like a horseshoe's been lying there, Vicky!' Carol said. 'Let's hope it means good luck for us!'

Smiling, Victoria went to the door and pressed the bell. In a moment it was opened by a young woman who curtly asked their business.

Carol looked at her with interest. Mabel Palmer was pretty in a rather heavy way. Her face would have been attractive if it hadn't been quite so surly. After all, though, she was having a rather a bad time . . . with her father dead, her sweetheart in prison . . .

Quickly, Victoria Lincoln handed over

her card, introduced Carol, and explained their business. As soon as Mabel realized they were anxious to help James Reynolds she held the door wide, asking them in.

Victoria was surprised to see the house so poorly furnished. The room which they entered contained only a strip of lino, a few wooden chairs and a small table on which reposed a vase full of flowers. They sat down. Mabel looked first at Carol, then at Victoria.

'Did Mr. Reynolds send you?'

'No — not exactly. We're working for a London newspaper — but we had a chat with Mr. Reynolds before we left. He — '

'I wonder what made him do it?' Mabel asked abruptly, almost as if Miss Lincoln hadn't spoken.

Caroline jumped at the sudden directness of the question.

'You think he's guilty, Miss Palmer?' she asked.

'Well — the police think so, don't they? Did he give you any message for me?'

Victoria nodded.

'He said: 'Tell Mabel I'm innocent.' That's all. As for me, Miss Palmer — I say he doesn't look like a thief and a murderer.'

She looked at the girl closely. Miss Palmer and the accused man had been more than friends; if Reynolds had stolen that money, he'd have done it for her sake as much as for his own. Therefore, if he was guilty, she would certainly know.

Her face remained expressionless though, almost sullen. It was quite obvious that she was unwilling — or unable — to help them. Miss Lincoln glanced casually round the room. A peculiar little thing about the vase of flowers attracted her attention.

The vase had been clumsily filled with a bunch of deep red roses; but in their midst was a large yellow sunflower. It looked oddly out of place.

'You're fond of flowers, Miss Palmer?' Victoria asked softly.

'I like them — yes.' She glanced at the vase without much interest.

'I was just thinking — the poor sunflower doesn't look very much at home amongst such noble company!'

Miss Lincoln spoke casually — but she

didn't take her eyes from Mabel's face. She saw a sudden flush stain the girl's cheeks, which paled just as quickly.

She looked ill at ease as she said:

'Oh, that's Mr. Benbow . . . he sent them up yesterday. He's the market gardener — his place is at the bottom of the Avenue. He must have been dreaming when he picked them!'

There was a pause. Then:

'Have you a photo of Mr. Reynolds?' Victoria asked.

'Yes. D'you want it?'

'If you don't mind, Miss Palmer. It would be a great help . . . '

She left the room to fetch it. This was just what Miss Lincoln wanted. She beckoned to Carol, told her to hold the vase while she pulled out the flowers. They came out bodily, all in a bunch, for they were tied roughly with a length of brown string.

'See this, Carol?' Victoria whispered excitedly. She pointed to the stems, which showed jagged, dirty edges. 'These flowers haven't been cut — they've been snatched hurriedly from their stalks! No market gardener would ever do *that*!'

Caroline nodded as Victoria replaced the bunch.

'But why should Miss Palmer tell a lie about who gave them to her?' Her voice was puzzled.

The detective raised a warning finger as Mabel's step sounded on the stairs. They were standing unconcernedly near the window when she came in with the photograph.

Ten minutes later, as they were walking back down the garden path, Caroline gripped her young employer's arm.

'The horseshoe, Vicky! There it is — on the edge of that border!'

Victoria looked. A rusty old horseshoe lay in the soft dirt bordering the path. As she bent to examine it, she spotted a piece of thin brown string attached to it.

Caroline saw it, too.

'It's the same kind that was used to tie up the flowers, isn't it?'

'Yes, my dear — I do believe it is.'

Thoughtfully, Victoria Lincoln straightened, gazed round the small garden. In the centre of the grass plot was a circular flowerbed with one flowerless rose tree, the leaves of which were drooping and brown. Victoria pointed.

'Let's have a look at that tree, Carol.'

They went over. The earth around it had been recently disturbed. The root of the tree sagged to one side where the soil hadn't been properly packed back.

Miss Lincoln said nothing. In fact, she was silent and deep in thought till they reached the end of the Avenue, where a board on a fence proclaimed:

'Albert Benbow,
        Market Gardener.'

Victoria leaned her arms on the fence, staring with narrowed eyes at the vista of greenhouses. Caroline waited patiently. She was beginning to understand the signs that denoted that her employer was intent on following up a line of investigation.

Miss Lincoln stood there so long that a man in a blue smock who'd been busy in one of the greenhouses came over.

'Anything I can do for you, ma'am?' he

asked, touching his cap respectfully.

'Yes — tell me why you included a sunflower in the bunch of roses you sent yesterday to Miss Palmer!'

The man scratched his head, his brows drawn.

'You're Mr. Benbow, I take it?' asked Victoria gravely. Briefly, she introduced herself and Carol and explained their business.

Mr. Benbow nodded. His puzzled frown deepened.

'Yes, ma'am — but I sent no flowers to Miss Palmer yesterday . . . or any other day! I'm not that well acquainted with the young lady!'

Here Carol, who'd been looking beyond the greenhouses to where flower-beds splashed in riotous collections of colours, touched her young employer's arm.

'Miss Lincoln — see over there? There's a rose garden . . . and against the wall near it, a bed of sunflowers!'

Victoria Lincoln nodded, her lips pursed primly.

'Good girl, Carol! See what I mean,

131

Mr. Benbow? Obviously Miss Palmer's flowers came from here — yet you say you know nothing about them?'

The gardener grinned suddenly.

'Ah — I think I can solve your little puzzle, though, Miss Lincoln! Constable Wetherall, now — he's a pal of mine — I've given him permission to come in here and pick flowers any time he likes. He takes them for his mother, who's an invalid — and I expect for Miss Palmer, too. He's supposed to be a bit sweet on her, I *do* know.'

'And he's on night duty this week, isn't he?' Carol said, quickly. 'I bet he passed here on his beat last night and decided to get some roses for Miss Palmer . . . and in the darkness he mixed a sunflower up with them!'

'You're dead on the target, my dear girl!' murmured the detective. 'And when he called at Number Four to deliver them, it was very late — so he tied them to the old horseshoe he found lying on the windowsill, no doubt adding a little love note. In the morning Miss Palmer finds them, cuts the horseshoe off and throws it on the garden.'

She nodded to Mr. Benbow.

'All right, sir — thanks very much for your assistance.' Then to Caroline: 'Come along, my dear . . . our jigsaw puzzle is nearly complete. Let's move quickly before the last piece runs away!'

Back in the High Street Miss Lincoln stopped at the first telephone booth and rang through to Mr. Desmond Carter.

An hour later, as dusk was falling, four plain-clothes policemen caught Miss Mabel Palmer in the act of digging two large suitcases from beneath the rose tree in the centre of her garden.

In them was the whole of the money stolen from the Farmers' National Bank!

*   *   *

The following morning the *Express and Star* editor listened in open admiration as Victoria Lincoln outlined the result of her investigations. Close to her sat Caroline Gerrard, hanging on to her every word.

'The whole thing becomes plain, Mr. Carter,' said the astute detective, 'when I tell you that Mr. Reynolds was being blackmailed by none other than Frederick Palmer — another ex-convict!'

'Not the night watchman?' asked the editor in amazement.

Miss Lincoln nodded.

'Yes, indeed — the anonymous letter writer was Fred Palmer. There's no doubt he'd planned this robbery of the bank very carefully, fixing everything so that Reynolds would be suspected. When he landed the night watchman's job there he made sure that Reynolds met his daughter. Her job was to gain Reynolds' confidence and learn all she could.

'So we come to the night of the robbery. When he read the letter that Reynolds had left for his employers, Palmer knew his blackmailing plan had succeeded. Reynolds had decided to clear out! Now was the time to act . . .

'He knew the exact times when Constable Wetherall passed the bank on his beat. So, watching his chance, when Wetherall was several streets away, he took Reynolds' keys from his desk, opened the strongroom, filled two big cases with the money and slipped across to his house — where he buried them beneath the rose tree in his garden. My assistant and I saw where it had been recently dug up. Now roses have thorns, Mr. Carter — that's where Palmer collected all those scratches on his hands!

'Then he hurried back to the bank. He'd prepared the tin of chloroform, the pad to place across his nose and mouth, the straps to bind his wrists and legs. Peeping from the side door, he waited till he saw Wetherall's lamp flashing at the top of Nayland Avenue. Then he ran inside, leaving the door ajar; he lay down beneath the punctured tin, tied the pad and strapping in place, knowing that Wetherall would arrive in a few moments, find the open door, and rescue him before he'd come to any great harm.

'Now we come to the spanner in the works!' Miss Lincoln smiled faintly. 'Constable Wetherall, it seems, had taken rather a fancy to Mabel Palmer. And as he passed the gardens of his friend Albert Benbow he thought it would be a nice idea to pick some roses for her and leave them at the house as he passed by.

'This he did — but it took some time, and while he was performing this act of kindness, the lady's unfortunate father was dying!

'You see what happened, Mr. Carter? A few moments after lying down Palmer would be unconscious. The chloroform would go on dripping; and when Wetherall eventually reached the bank, nearly twenty minutes after he was due, the man was dead!'

Desmond Carter leaned back, gazing for a long moment at Victoria's calmly smiling face.

'It's really marvellous!' he murmured. 'How on earth you began on this case — how you found your first ideas . . . well, it beats me!'

Victoria Lincoln laughed.

'It's my criminal mind, Mr. Carter! I see the most awful clues in the most innocent things . . . in rose trees, in scratches on a man's hand, in bits of string, in sunflowers . . . even in lucky horseshoes!'

3

THE KIDNAPPED
RETRIEVER

Victoria Lincoln slipped her latchkey into the door of her flat and stepped into the hall.

Humming softly, she went to her study, palmed the handle, and entered. Next second she sprang aside as a large shape leapt out at her.

'Well, for Heaven's sake!' she exclaimed.

Her mysterious 'assailant' was a big brown retriever, a lovely dog with a glossy coat, flapping ears, and shining, friendly eyes. As Victoria spoke the dog gave a deep bark. At a glance the young detective saw that he wore no collar.

'Old boy, unless you came down the chimney, I don't see how on earth you came in. The only other person with a key to this flat is Carol — and she's away on holiday. Is somebody playing a joke on me?'

She went round the room carefully, searching for a note of some kind — but found nothing. Then the dog began to bark and whine eagerly. Recognising the symptoms Victoria went to the kitchen, found the remains of the cold joint and left the retriever ravenously munching the bone.

'Let's see,' she murmured, 'I left about eleven this morning . . . it's now six-thirty; and from the way that dog is wolfing the meat I should imagine he's been here several hours. The thing is: who brought him — and how, and why?'

She broke off, staring sharply at the blotter on the desk. To the ordinary eye nothing was amiss; but Victoria's trained observation noted a seemingly unimportant trifle. Apparently the fire had been smoking during her absence, for a film of smuts covered the desktop and blotter. On the blotter, however, was a faintly marked oblong patch over which the smuts had not fallen!

Victoria bent, examined it closely. A tingle of excitement ran through her as she discovered a pinprick in the blotting paper, just at the top of the patch. 'So a note *was* left for me after all!' she muttered grimly. 'And for some reason it's been removed. Ah! I thought as much!'

Her sharp eyes had caught a tiny gleam from the carpet. She bent, picked up a pin — an imitation gold one obviously snapped from a brooch or tie-pin. Victoria fastened it in her lapel, then stood staring at the desk. Why had the note been removed — and by whom? Had the writer changed his or her mind? Or had someone else entered the flat later?

Victoria chuckled. 'Seems there's been quite a little party here this afternoon. Folks coming and going and leaving notes and dogs and what-not. What the dickens is it all about?'

Then her attention became fixed on the wall behind the desk. Plainly visible here were several deep scratches. Could they have been made by the dog leaping up? Victoria wondered — for immediately above was the ventilator. Then her keen eyes noted something else; quickly she pulled up a chair and jumped on it to investigate. Her eyes glinted as she discovered a segment of torn paper; she was further elated to see that, printed on it, was the tail end of two words . . . HT and . . . EL.

Victoria took her find back to the desk, sat down, her brow furrowed in thought. The picture was becoming a little clearer now. A note had been pinned to the blotter by the person who had in some way brought the dog into the flat. Then later someone else had come up the fire escape, perhaps to reconnoitre . . . and, through the ventilator, had fished out the note with a piece of wire, tearing off a corner of the notepaper in the process. The dog had seen him and had jumped up at the ventilator.

Reaching up, she took a bulky guide-book from the shelf, scanned painstakingly through a long list of London hotels — for she'd decided that the second word on the torn paper was 'hotel'. There were several Connaught Hotels; and to begin with she chose the one nearest her flat, in Verner Street.

She jumped up, reached for her hat, called the dog. Obediently, it bounded in from the kitchen. Victoria found a luggage strap, fastened it round the animal's neck for a collar. Twenty minutes later, with the retriever straining at the improvised leash, she stood outside the Connaught in Verner Street, She saw that it was an old-fashioned type of family hotel; and if the dog's excitement meant anything, Victoria told herself she'd hit the bull's eye first time.

Through the hotel's large ground-floor window she could see a comfortable lounge. At a small table sat a beautiful, fair-haired girl playing cards with a stout, baldish, shifty-faced gentleman and a thin, acid-countenanced female. After a moment, the girl looked up, saw Miss Lincoln and the dog. Immediately, it seemed, she made some excuse to her companions, rose, and left the room.

From the sudden strained look on the girl's face the lady detective realised that here was something not quite on the level. The dog now was straining impatiently to reach the hotel steps. Victoria gave him his head, following thoughtfully. As she entered the lobby the first person she encountered was the lovely blonde girl.

The retriever struggled frantically at its leash as they came face to face. Then Miss Lincoln's dark eyes flashed as she smiled, extending her hand.

'Caroline Gerrard, of all people! I never expected to bump unto you here . . . You're supposed to be on a week's holiday with your parents, aren't you?'

'I can understand you being puzzled, Miss Lincoln! I can explain everything though, honestly — '

'Carol — this is your dog, isn't it?' Victoria broke in. 'You came to my flat this afternoon and left it there. What was the idea? And why are you back in London? In other words — suppose you tell me what all this is about?'

'Well, I'd only been home a couple of days when my Uncle George asked Mum if I could spend the rest of the week here with him and his friends — Mr. and Mrs, Nelson, those two people I was playing cards with. The day before yesterday Uncle George had to pop off unexpectedly to Scotland on some urgent business or other, and I don't expect him back till Saturday. I — '

She paused. Victoria shrugged. All this fast talk told her nothing. What was Caroline getting at, she wondered? Also, she still wanted to know why the dog had been left at her flat . . .

'Well, Carol? I'm still in the dark as to the reason for your extraordinary behaviour. Can you — ?'

Caroline caught the detective's arm, drew her into the lounge, told the waiter to bring coffee. When they were seated, she leaned forward, speaking eagerly.

'Look, Vicky, I came round to your flat today to see you. I'd phoned for you at your office earlier this morning. Pamela said you were out on a case, but that you'd told her you'd be returning to your flat this afternoon.'

Victoria nodded. 'That's right, only I got back somewhat later than I'd planned — '

'I had Ranger with me when I called to see you because I was terrified for him. When I found you were still out I let myself in with the key you'd given me, and left Ranger there for safety. I wrote you a note explaining everything — didn't you get it?'

'Someone else came up, by the fire escape — and hooked your note out somehow. What's the idea, Carol? Why are you so worried about the dog? He seems a sensible sort of chap to me.' She bent down, patted Ranger, who was lying placidly beneath the table.

'Oh, Ranger is okay so long as he is left in peace; it's these Nelson people, Miss Lincoln — I'm certain they're out to do him harm. It only started after Uncle George left — but gosh, I'm frightened for Ranger's life! Morning before last old Nelson was standing over the road there, whistling Ranger to come out of the hotel and across the street — with cars and lorries streaming by, mind you! Ranger would have gone, too, if I hadn't come down just at that minute and called him back. They've put poisoned meat in his kennel — I'm certain it was them. They've used every trick they can think of to get him away from me and to a vet so they can try and have him destroyed. I'm not letting him out of my sight for one

146

second — no fear!'

The lady detective listened patiently. 'Pardon me if I say that your suspicions seem rather easily aroused, Carol. Why should . . . ?'

'Ah, I forgot to tell you that!' Carol cut in. 'You see, Ranger belonged to my Aunt Claribel, but she died a few weeks ago and since then Uncle George has looked after him. I tell you, he's been very particular about the job, too! Why, before he went to Scotland he told me to guard the dog with my *life* — that on no account must anything happen to him. You understand now? I was so scared for his safety I came to see you — but you weren't there, so I left Ranger, knowing he'd be safe for a while, till I could see you and arrange what was to be done. Can you help me, Miss Lincoln?'

Victoria sipped her coffee thoughtfully.

'The fact that your note was taken from my desk proves that someone followed you to my place; and *that* proves that there's more in this case than meets the eye! From your story I should say that Mr. Nelson is the one to watch. For some reason best known to himself he wants Ranger out of the way — while your Uncle George is just as eager to keep him unharmed. Yes, I think I can help you, Carol. You must keep Ranger here! He's the decoy, you see — the bait which will lure the crook or crooks into the open and give us a chance to work. There's something behind it all, I'm certain of that; and I'm quite keen to find out just what it is!'

'I'm tremendously grateful to you, Miss Lincoln. Shall we plan our campaign right away?'

'Well, during the day *you're* on guard — eh? I doubt if Ranger's enemies will attempt anything further in daylight, anyway. I imagine they're convinced by now that they'll never get past you. No — night time is what we have to watch. Leave Ranger in his usual place tonight — where does he sleep, by the way?'

'His kennel's in the yard.'

'All right, I'll be there, on the watch.'

Walking back to her flat the young detective felt pleasurably excited over this peculiar case. Her keen instinct, which rarely failed her, warned her that strange things would be happening before long. Those things, she was convinced, would centre on the brown retriever!

*   *   *

Shortly after eleven that night Victoria Lincoln pulled on a heavy coat, wound a muffler round her neck, and set off from her flat to Verner Street. Straight to the yard at the rear of the Connaught Hotel she made her way. She soon found Ranger, moving restlessly at the end of a long chain. The dog knew her instantly and Victoria had difficulty in restraining its eager barks of welcome. 'Quiet now, Ranger! Lie down, there's a good chap . . . lie down!'

Presently the dog subsided obediently, lying quietly with its head between its paws. The detective sat down on a rough bench beside the small shed that did duty as Ranger's kennel.

Time passed. Midnight tolled from a nearby church tower.

Next moment the dog's excited whines

jerked Miss Lincoln from her thoughts. She shone her torch inside the small door. There was Ranger worrying at a pile of straw in one corner. In a few seconds the dog had pulled out a large lump of meat attached to a bone. It was hard work for Victoria to get it out of Ranger's mouth! For the detective had noticed a strong, unpleasant smell coming from the meat; also strange discolourations on it showed up in the revealing light from her torch. What Caroline had said was true. Some scoundrel had planted this poison stuff especially for Ranger to find . . .

There was a grim look in Victoria Lincoln's eye as she wrapped the evil-smelling meat in a sheet of old newspaper. Ranger whined his disappointment. Patting his head Victoria said:

'Sorry, old boy — but there's nothing doing. There's some funny business going on here — and I'm not resting till I find out what it is.'

Up till now she hadn't taken Caroline Gerrard's story completely seriously. But this discovery had shocked her unpleasantly. Someone had sinister intentions towards the amiable Ranger. Why? Obviously the dog was everyone's friend. Why should anyone wish him harm? The whole thing was the more interesting to Victoria because it was so inexplicable.

They sat in silence as the peace of night crept over the city. Gradually the hours dragged by and the detective dozed but with one eye open! Four booming strokes sounded from a distant church clock. Victoria jerked up then as she heard Ranger's chain clank. Was that a stealthy step from the black shadow of the far wall?

Straining her ears the detective fancied she heard shuffling. Ranger began to rumble deep in his throat. Revolver in hand, Victoria edged softly across to the wall dividing the hotel yard from a rear alley.

Maybe the sound had come from behind the wall . . . Victoria drew herself up, flashed her torch down into the alley. At that moment something caught her a stunning blow on the back of her head. She slid down the wall, losing consciousness before she hit the ground.

* ★ ★

A grey, chill dawn was breaking when the detective opened her eyes. She felt shivery cold and her head throbbed wretchedly. By painful degrees she collected her scattered senses, struggled to her knees.

'Ranger — Ranger!' she shouted.

There was no answering bark from the shed. Cold silence greeted her frenzied calls. Then she drew in her breath sharply, as a glance towards the shed door confirmed her worst fears. Ranger's chain dangled loosely there . . . one of its links had been sawn through!

Miss Lincoln's lips tightened. A brief inspection of the yard revealed nothing, so she hurried back into the hotel. In the lobby she roused the drowsy night porter.

'Mr. Gerrard's dog, Ranger — that big brown retriever in the yard . . . have you seen him?'

'Eh? Ranger? Yes . . . isn't he in his kennel, Ma'am?'

'No — he's vanished. He's been stolen during the night.'

As she spoke, a startled cry sounded

behind her. An elderly, kindly-faced gentleman had just pushed through the swing door of the hotel followed by a peak-capped chauffeur carrying luggage.

'Are you talking about Ranger?' he gasped. 'Don't tell me any harm has come to him?'

'Sorry, sir — your dog's been stolen, I'm afraid. You're Mr. Gerrard, I presume?' Then when the old man nodded: 'Tell me — is Ranger of any considerable value? So many folks seem to be very interested in him!'

Mr. Gerrard's eyes narrowed.

'That doesn't matter now. He was left to me by a very dear friend who died recently — and he must be found! I want him brought back to me — alive and well. Who are you, anyway?' he asked, looking closely at Victoria Lincoln.

Victoria handed over her card. Mr. Gerrard's face brightened a little.

'Ah — a lady detective, eh? All right, young woman — you've a job. You find Ranger and get him back here unharmed — and I'll pay you anything you ask.' Beckoning his chauffeur, he walked across to the stairs, muttering: 'Silly fool I was to go away and leave him here . . .'

The old man's words had whetted anew her desire to solve this mystery, which had been appreciably deepened by yet another party on the scene who was vitally interested in the dog's welfare!

From the porter she was given the number of Carol's room, then went to wake her. Over breakfast she related briefly the exciting events of the night.

'You'll be glad to know your Uncle has returned, Carol. He knows Ranger's missing — and he's terribly upset. We simply must find that dog!'

Carol gulped down her toast and marmalade.

'I'm ready when you are, Miss Lincoln! I suppose you're going to look for clues now?'

'That's right. Where do you suggest we start?'

'Oh — I don't know. How about . . . well, the yard, I should think, would be a good place. Those people who took Ranger may — '

Victoria nodded, patted Carol's hand on the table.

'You're a smart girl, my dear! The yard — and especially around Ranger's shed — *is* undoubtedly the best place to start. So let's go!'

They went back to the yard, searching minutely for any clue, however trivial. On the shed floor Carol made the first discovery — some white, powdery substance on the boards. Rubbing a little between forefinger and thumb, Victoria decided that it was flour. Didn't this point to a sack? Ranger had been carried away in a sack.

'What about a flour sack, Carol? Ranger may have been whisked away in a flour sack — and that suggests a mill, or bakery. D'you know of one near here?'

'Yes, I do!' Carol spoke excitedly. 'If we go out through the yard door, turn left down the alley, then left again at the bottom, we'll see an old flour warehouse right in front.'

'Then it sounds a very likely spot!' said Victoria Lincoln. 'It's our next stop, Carol.'

They sped out into the alley. Five minutes later they were staring up at the warehouse, which seemed completely deserted.

'Why, it's an ideal place to hide Ranger!' exclaimed Miss Lincoln. 'And I'll wager that's just what those scoundrels who took him are doing — till darkness falls and he can be safely disposed of. Carol, we're getting in there . . . by hook or by crook!'

Carol trembled with excitement as they made a quick tour of the building; in a narrow, weed-grown lane at the rear they found a rusty chain dangling from some kind of derrick. A quick leap, a strong pull — and Victoria found herself in a dim, dusty loft. She knelt, leaned over, gave Carol a hand up.

Heavy cobwebs and the thick dirt of long disuse clustered all about them. Grimy flour sacks lay all around on the floor. And presently Victoria felt her scalp tingle as one, bulkier than the rest and heaped up in a corner, moved.

She sprang towards it, and with her pocket knife ripped it open. Inside was

Ranger — securely bound and muzzled, but unharmed!

★ ★ ★

Back in his room at the hotel, Mr. George Gerrard sat talking to his friend, the bald-headed Howard Nelson. Nelson was rubbing his hands, pacing up and down the floor.

'Well, George — it looks as though you won't get Claribel's money after all — eh?'

The old man's face paled.

'What on earth do you mean?'

'Ah — you think I don't know, eh? Aunt Clarrie made a will, didn't she? You get all her money — providing Ranger is alive and well two years after her death! *I've* a solicitor too, George. He made a few enquiries, and told me the news. If anything happens to Ranger before that time is up — the money comes to me!'

Mr. Gerrard stared out of the window, clenching and unclenching his hands.

'Howard . . . you don't think . . . you promised to look after Ranger while I was away. You said you'd help Caroline to see no harm came to him. You — '

'Well, so I did. Good heavens, the dog will be all right. You wouldn't expect me to sit up with him all night, surely? He's just broken his chain and gone off for a run somewhere, that's all. But, if he *does* meet with an accident . . . well, it'll be bad luck on you, George — won't it?'

Mr. Gerrard was about to answer when someone knocked on the door. Next second it opened — to admit Victoria Lincoln!

'Mr. Gerrard — your dog is safe! Someone knocked me out during the night and kidnapped him. Your niece and I found him trussed up in a sack in that old warehouse down the alley.'

In a few words Mr. Gerrard expressed his fervent thanks and acquainted Victoria with the strange facts of the case. Meanwhile, Howard Nelson had slumped in a chair, his plump face going a dirty grey colour.

'What do you think happened, Miss Lincoln?' asked Mr. Gerrard.

'It's fairly simple, sir. Someone wanted

that dog removed. And I've a good idea who it is. Her meaning glance at Nelson didn't pass unnoticed by Mr. Gerrard. 'That person has made several attempts to kill Ranger whilst you've been away. In fact, your niece became so worried that yesterday she brought the dog to me for safekeeping. I was out, so she left Ranger in my flat, with a note on my desk explaining things. This same someone obviously had followed her — for the note was removed from my desk just so I wouldn't know whose dog it was. I expect they hoped then that I'd have it destroyed!

'But this plan failed — and last night the scheming scoundrel became really desperate. He paid two men to kidnap the dog in the early hours, and do away with it; but as it was getting light they apparently decided to keep Ranger tied up till night time, when they could drop him in the river with a few bricks tied to him. Neat idea, eh?'

'How do you know all this?'

'All — truth will out, sir! An old lady who has a room opposite the warehouse

159

saw these two men taking the sack with Ranger in it, into the warehouse about four-thirty this morning. I've already spoken to her. She *knows* the men, sir — she says they used to work at the warehouse. I've given the police their descriptions, and the district where they live — the old girl knew that, too. They'll be picked up soon — perhaps this morning, and when they are, they'll talk all right . . . they always do! *Then* we'll find out who paid them to kill Ranger!'

There was a sudden scrape as Howard Nelson shoved back his chair. With dragging steps he crossed to the door, went out without a word.

'If the cap fits . . . ' murmured Victoria.

Then Mr. Gerrard understood.

'Good heavens!' he gasped. 'You mean — Howard? Why, of course — why didn't I realise that before?'

'If, as you say, he gets all your Aunt's money if anything happens to Ranger — I'd keep him and the dog just as far apart as you can, sir! He's a crook, if you ask me!'

'I understand everything now, Miss

160

Lincoln and I've only you to thank for it! I think you've done a very smart piece of work.'

'Well — you must thank Caroline too, sir. If it hadn't been for her astuteness I'd never have known about the case at all.'

Mr. Gerrard's blue eyes twinkled.

'She's a smart girl all right, that niece of mine.' Pulling out a wallet, he thumbed through a thick wad of notes. 'Now — name your fee, Miss Lincoln!'

Victoria murmured: 'I leave it to you, sir . . . '

Ten minutes later, her arms affectionately squeezing Carol's shoulders, Victoria Lincoln stood outside the Connaught Hotel and hailed a taxi.

'Your Uncle George has been very generous, Carol! You and I are going out to paint the old town a lovely deep red!'

4

MURDER AT GREYSTONES LODGE

On Saturday afternoon, on their way back from a successful case in Somerset, Victoria Lincoln decided to stop at the little town of Newbury, in Berkshire.

'The police inspector there is an old friend of mine, Carol,' she told her young assistant. Tom Hadleigh and I have worked on several cases together. I shouldn't like to ride through without saying Hello.'

Caroline nodded her blonde head, smiling.

'Okay, Miss Lincoln. That's what I like about this job — we're always meeting fresh people, seeing new places.' She turned admiring eyes to her employer. 'I'm just beginning to realise how lucky I am to be working with you, Miss Lincoln! When I think of some of the stuffy old jobs I *might* have gone into . . . ugh!'

Victoria's dark eyes flashed in a quick smile as she patted Carol's arm. 'I'm glad you're happy, dear. As for me — I'm more than satisfied with your work. Never forget that what distinguishes the well-trained detective from the ordinary person is his or her ability to observe small details that wouldn't be noticed by other people. See the idea? Remember: always be on the watch for the small things — for the seemingly insignificant trifles will very often lead to a valuable clue.'

Presently they came to the sleepy little town. Miss Lincoln steered the car slowly down the narrow, bustling High Street, crowded with weekend shoppers. At the bottom was the police station — a snug, greystone building, squatting in the centre of a concreted yard. Victoria pulled in, stopped the engine; she stepped out, stretching gratefully.

Caroline followed her into the Inspector's office. Tom Hadleigh sat at his desk chatting to a powerfully-built young man with a mop of carroty hair. Both jumped up as the two young women entered.

'Well, if it isn't Vicky Lincoln!' said Hadleigh, holding out his hand. 'Always pleased to see *your* smiling face, young woman! What brings you to our little haven of rest, eh?'

Victoria smiled.

'On our way back to town, Tom. We've been on a case in the country. I couldn't pass through without popping in to see you.'

'I should think not, indeed!' Hadleigh grinned at Caroline. 'And who's your friend?'

'Ah, that's Miss Gerrard, Tom — Caroline Gerrard, my assistant. Carol, my dear, meet Inspector Hadleigh — you'll find him a very staunch friend, I know.'

'Pleased to know you, Miss Gerrard.' Carol and Hadleigh shook hands. Then the Inspector nodded to the young man. 'And this is Keith Gregory — he's a reporter from our local paper.'

When the introductions were complete Miss Lincoln turned to Keith.

'I expect you find things a little slow here, Mr. Gregory?'

'Hell, yes! I get bored to death with it sometimes, believe me ... especially when I think of the fun and excitement I used to get, working with the big London dailies! Murders, smash-and-grabs, daring robberies, fires . . . everything a reporter could wish for! But *here* . . . nothing ever seems to happen.'

Victoria wondered why he'd left London at all, if he'd liked it so much. In fact, she was just going to ask him why he'd come down to Newbury to work, when the 'phone bell shrilled. She glanced at Carol, then nodded towards the clock. Together they noted the time. It was just twenty minutes to three.

Hadleigh reached for the receiver,

'Yes . . . Police station here. Who? Ah . . . you've just discovered it? Right . . . we'll be out there right away!'

He slammed back the 'phone, jumped up. 'Here's something in your line, folks! Old Roger Renworthy, of Greystones Lodge, has just been found dead in his study! There's been a terrific struggle, the manservant says. It looks like murder — so come on!'

Keith was up in a flash and making for the door.

'Greystones Lodge, eh?' he jerked out.

'Thanks, Inspector — a lucky break at last!'

Before the Inspector could give any order to his own men he'd jumped on his motorbike and was roaring off down the street.

Hadleigh grinned, looking at Miss Lincoln and Carol.

'Like to come along, ladies? It promises to be quite exciting!'

'That's what we're looking for Tom — excitement with a capital E!' Victoria rejoined. 'What d'you say, Carol?'

'Definitely!'

The Inspector rang for his sergeant, who came in almost immediately — a stolid, dark-haired man named Bill Henley.

'Bill — we're off to Greystones Lodge,' Hadleigh announced. 'Get the car right away and let's be moving.'

The Lodge, it appeared, lay well out of town on the Guildford road, but the drive entrance was down a lane that wasn't at all easy to find. There was hardly a soul about from whom they could get directions. So by the time they arrived at the Lodge — which was a large old-fashioned building let off from two flats — Keith Gregory had been there for some time, and was busy making notes and taking pictures. He showed them into a ground floor front room. 'The old boy's in here, Inspector . . . '

Roger Kenworthy, a huge, burly man was lying twisted in an armchair. All the stuff in the room was topsy-turvy. Obviously, there'd been a desperate struggle. The radio lay on its side in a corner, glasses and a decanter from the broken table lay smashed on the floor, three small chairs were overturned, and the carpet was in an awful mess. A torn curtain flapped at the open window. Miss Lincoln went up to Keith, who was scribbling away in his notebook.

'You're sure nothing's been touched?' she asked.

'Absolutely, ma'am! I know better than that. Everything's exactly as I found it.'

Victoria turned to the dead man's servant, who'd let them in. He was a thin, under-sized little man, named Darrell.

170

'You're the one who telephoned, Mr. Darrell?'

'Yes, ma'am. I'd just been out shopping. When I came back I found the master — like this . . . '

Hadleigh and Sergeant Henley made a brief examination of the body. Kenworthy's throat was swollen and badly bruised and one of his eyes was blackened. He'd been strangled, and he'd put up a furious fight for his life.

Victoria Lincoln nudged her young assistant. 'There's something to notice, Carol . . . Whoever killed him must be as strong as an ox. Kenworthy was at least six feet three in height and he'd weigh sixteen stones easily.'

Caroline nodded as the Inspector went to the 'phone, called up the police station. Miss Lincoln went back to the reporter.

'Mr. Gregory — you must have been one of the first people on the spot after the murder?'

'Well, yes, ma'am — next to Darrell, I suppose I was.'

'H'mm. Did you see anyone about — I mean any suspicious characters? Either in the house, or in the lane?'

He thought for a moment, then his eyes narrowed.

'Now you mention it, Miss Lincoln — I did! There's a field at the rear of the house, and from the hall window I saw a man crossing it. I reckoned he'd be a workman — they're building some new houses further down the lane.'

'I see. Could you manage a description of this man?'

'Well, hardly Miss Lincoln. He was smoking a pipe, though, because he stopped to light it, and — '

He broke off as Julian Paget, the police surgeon, bustled in. He made a rapid but thorough examination of the body.

'Cause of death was dislocation of the neck,' he announced presently. 'Plus choking and strangulation caused by heavy pressure of human fingers.'

'Then whoever did it is an abnormally strong man?' Victoria asked.

'Undoubtedly.'

Paget packed his bag and left. Hadleigh 'phoned the hospital, told them to collect the body. Then he ordered Henley to dust the room thoroughly for fingerprints. While he did this Victoria further questioned Darrell, who limped slightly when he walked and was obviously a frail old man.

'How long have you worked for Mr. Kenworthy, Darrell?'

'Nearly six years, ma'am.'

'D'you know if he had any enemies?'

'Can't say, ma'am. I know he had something to do with newspaper publishing, but — '

'Yes . . . h'mm . . . was he a rich man?'

'Always seemed so, ma'am. Many's the time he's promised I'd be well provided for if anything happened to him. But, of course, I won't know about that till the will is read.'

'I see. Well, Darrell, as you've been with him for such a long time, I gather you always found him a good employer? Even-tempered, reasonable?'

'Yes indeed, ma'am.'

'And who lives in the flat upstairs?'

'Young lady by the name of Marlowe — Ethel Marlowe. She's secretary to a doctor in the city.'

'Have you seen her this afternoon? I mean, is she here now?'

'Yes, ma'am. I went up and told her what had happened. I knew she'd be in. Saturday is her off-day.'

While Hadleigh and the Inspector finished their inspection of the room, Victoria and Caroline went upstairs to interview Ethel Marlowe. She was a pretty, slim girl, with a delicately rounded face.

Miss Lincoln introduced herself and Carol, and explained their business.

'I was wondering if you'd heard the noise of the struggle, Miss Marlowe,' Victoria asked. 'It's fairly obvious Mr. Kenworthy fought gallantly before he was overcome. Can you help us in that direction?'

The girl shrugged.

'I heard a thump or two, certainly. I just thought Mr. Kenworthy was moving a chair or something, though. Then again, he had the radio on very loud. I was listening out for that especially you see, Miss Lincoln ... my favourite band, the Kentucky Rythmagicians, was just coming on. I heard them play their signature tune — then suddenly the radio was switched off and — '

'Pardon me, Miss Marlowe — you have no radio of your own?'

'No, miss — I always listened to Mr. Kenworthy's. But, as I say, when he switched it off, as I thought, I just shut my door and didn't bother any more. There seemed to be a bit more noise after that, for a minute or two — then everything went quiet.'

They chatted for a short while, but Victoria soon realised that Ethel Marlowe knew very little of Kenworthy's character or of his affairs. They went downstairs again. Henley, who was finishing his examination of the room, beckoned them over to the radio. He pointed to where the flex leading to the switch was broken. 'Became tangled up in their feet during the struggle, eh, Miss Lincoln,' he said.

Caroline realised then what Ethel Marlowe meant when she'd said Kenworthy suddenly had turned off his radio. He hadn't *turned* it off at all. The wire had been broken as he'd fought for his life . . .

Suddenly her scalp tingled. Her fingers clenched and unclenched as she developed that tremendously exciting feeling familiar to all detectives. She'd stumbled across something that didn't fit in! In other words, she'd found a clue . . .

She turned to the piano, picked up a newspaper lying there. At the back of her mind was running the thought that the Kentucky Rhythmagicians were a regular Saturday afternoon broadcast. Their music was relayed from a dance hall, where they played for a tea dance . . . they always came on dead on three o'clock! And she knew dance bands always began their programme with their signature tune . . .

Yet Miss Marlowe emphatically had stated that she'd heard that signature tune while the struggle in Kenworthy's room was actually in progress! In other words, that meant that Kenworthy was very much alive at twenty to three — when Darrell had 'phoned up to say he was dead!

Hurriedly she found the radio programmes in the paper. Her memory hadn't failed her. At three o'clock that very afternoon the Kentucky Rythmagicians had commenced their usual broadcast from the Ashford Palais de Dance!

Victoria Lincoln's eyes glowed with praise when Caroline told her about this.

'Grand work, Carol, my dear! That's what I call real smart deduction. You're learning very quickly.'

Carol was thrilled to death. After all, it was a supreme moment in her life. She'd discovered her first clue.

'Doesn't this put Darrell under suspicion, Miss Lincoln?' she breathed. 'That's silly though, really — isn't it? How could a frail creature like him possibly have struggled with a big, strong man like Mr. Kenworthy?'

Miss Lincoln shook her head.

'It's certainly a puzzle for the moment, Carol. One thing seems certain — Darrell hasn't been telling the complete truth. By the way — I wonder if Keith Gregory's still here? Slip out and see, will you?'

In five minutes Caroline returned with the young reporter. Keith said:

'I was just off, Miss. Did you want me?'

Miss Lincoln told him of Carol's discovery, and what it implied. He sat down, lit a cigarette. He scratched his head, said:

'Now there's a might funny how-de-do, eh?'

'It certainly is,' Victoria agreed. 'By the way, did you know Mr. Kenworthy at all, Mr. Gregory?'

'Me? Why, no. Can't say I've set eyes on him till today.'

Half an hour later, Inspector Hadleigh, Sergeant Henley, Miss Lincoln and Caroline were driving back to town.

'The only thing that might give us any kind of a lead now is Roger Kenworthy's will,' Victoria said. 'I've had a look through his papers. His solicitors are Peters and Heap, of Lincoln's Inn, London. Will you ring up Mr. Peters at his home, Tom? He may be able to tell us something.'

Back at the police station Inspector Hadleigh consulted the London 'phone directory. After a long wait he contacted Mr. Peters at his home address. He signalled to Victoria, who went over, bent her head to the receiver.

Hadleigh said:

'Newbury Police here, Mr. Peters — Inspector Hadleigh speaking. A client of yours . . . a Mr. Roger Kenworthy, of Greystones Lodge, has been murdered. To help our investigations, will you please tell us something about his will?'

There was a pause. Victoria heard the solicitor clear his throat, then he said:

'How dreadful! Roger Kenworthy? Good heavens . . . what a terrible thing! Er, just a moment, Inspector. I'll have to go to my safe.'

When he returned he said:

'The bulk of Kenworthy's money goes to his sister, who's in Canada.'

'Yes . . . and how about his servant — Darrell?'

'Ah — just a moment . . . yes, he gets a thousand pounds.'

'Thank you very much, sir. That's very interesting. I — '

He paused as Miss Lincoln nudged his arm. She whispered:

'Ask him which newspaper Kenworthy was interested in.'

Hadleigh nodded, bent again to the 'phone.

'Just one thing more, Mr. Peters. I understand Mr. Kenworthy had an interest in one or two newspapers. Can you tell me which ones?'

'Certainly. He owned the *Evening Courier*, and was part owner of the *Daily Record*.'

As Hadleigh hung up the receiver Victoria Lincoln whispered quietly to her assistant:

'I think we're getting somewhere, Carol! Both those papers are well known London ones . . . '

Aloud, she said to inspector Hadleigh:

'Tom, I have another idea. Will you ring up Mr. Kenworthy's papers, and ask the editors if they've heard of a Keith Gregory, a reporter? I should try the *Courier* first.'

'All right, Vicky. I can see you're on to something!'

He rang through to the *Courier* office without any trouble. Again Victoria listened in to the conversation. She heard the editor say, in answer to Hadleigh's question about Keith Gregory:

''I have, Inspector. He used to work for this paper — he's also worked for the *Record*. Mr. Kenworthy blacklisted him, along with all the other London editors too. He'll never get another newspaper job in London!'

'Ah, I see! I'm very much obliged for your help . . . '

There was a tense silence as the Inspector rang off. Caroline said:

'No wonder he'd told us he'd never seen Mr. Kenworthy before, Miss Lincoln!'

Sergeant Henley broke in: 'Well, that gives us two people with a motive for killing Kenworthy! Supposing Darrell had found out he was getting a thousand quid when his boss died? He'd want to get his hands on the money quickly — wouldn't he? And Gregory — well, he imagined he'd a grudge against the old boy . . . '

Inspector Hadleigh nodded.

'Two suspects, Sergeant, as you say — but both with well-nigh perfect alibis! It was a physical impossibility for Darrell to have done the job — he hasn't the strength to hold a child. While Gregory was in this office when the message came through about Kenworthy's death. He'd been chatting with me a good half hour before that, too.'

'Yes — but how about Miss Marlowe's evidence?' Victoria said quietly. 'If *her* story is true Kenworthy was still fighting for his life at three o'clock! So what d'you make of that?'

She jumped up. 'I've worked a little idea out, Inspector. Keith Gregory told me where he lives. I think we'll go and have a little talk with him. Come on . . .'

Gregory lodged with an old lady called Palmer in a little house just outside the town. They found him in a shed in the back garden, tinkering with his motor-bike. Hadleigh didn't waste any time.

'Mr. Gregory,' he said, 'did you tell Miss Lincoln that Mr. Kenworthy was a complete stranger to you?'

He looked a bit startled.

'Sure. Why, what's wrong?'

'Just this. I've discovered you used to work for him and that he sacked you for dishonesty! He also made it impossible for you to work on any other London paper. Is that right?'

Gregory went red as fire, then as quickly his face paled.

'Well, yes, Inspector . . . but I've a decent job now and I didn't want anyone to know I'd been such a fool. That's all.'

'I see. You understand, Mr. Gregory — my job is to explore every angle of this case. For instance, it struck me that you might have hated Kenworthy enough to follow him down here and murder him. It also struck me that Darrell, if he'd known just how much his employer had left him, might have desired Kenworthy's early death, too. See the idea? I must leave no stone unturned to — '

'Are you suggesting I murdered Kenworthy?' exploded the reporter. 'Good heavens, I was sitting talking to you when the damned murder was committed! Don't talk such nonsense, inspector!'

'Ah! Just a minute!' Victoria spoke quietly. 'I agree you were at the police station when the message came through from Darrell. That's not the same thing at all! When Darrell 'phoned, Kenworthy was alive and well. He was sitting in his armchair, with the radio going full blast. Ah, we've a reliable witness, Gregory — don't worry about that. The same witness states that at ten to three you arrived on your motorbike; you were let in by Darrell, and you went straight to Kenworthy's room. *Then* it was that the murder took place! You and Darrell planned it between you! He 'phoned at twenty to three, knowing you were sitting in the inspector's office — just to provide you with a cast-iron alibi!'

She made a sudden sign to Hadleigh, who whipped out a pair of handcuffs.

'But it hasn't worked, Gregory. We're going to arrest you for the murder of Roger Kenworthy! Take him, Inspector!'

Victoria's little bluff worked to perfection. Gregory snatched up a heavy spanner and dived at Hadleigh. His one idea was to make a wild dash for freedom.

He didn't succeed, though. Sergeant Henley happened to be the Southern Counties Heavyweight Champion! His right fist shot out and it landed on Gregory's jaw. There was a crack like a thick piece of wood snapping. Gregory went down with a crash and he stayed down.

Half an hour later he was safely locked up and making a full confession.

★ ★ ★

That night Victoria and Carol stayed at the Falcon Hotel in Newbury. Over supper the detective was full of praise for her clever assistant.

'Remember what I told you about noticing the little things, Carol . . . how they often helped to solve a mystery? Well — it happened in the Kenworthy case, didn't it? Henley noticed the radio flex was broken — and you connected that with the other little detail about the Kentucky Rythmagicians coming on at three o'clock prompt. You carry on like this, my dear — and I'm sure you'll be famous one day!'

She leaned back, took out a small box of milk chocolates from her handbag, offered it to Carol and took one for herself.

'I'm *very* proud of my new assistant . . . ' Victoria said softly.

5

MY SON IS INNOCENT

One glance around his study showed Andrew Holmes that all was not as it should be.

Papers littered the floor, cushions were in disarray, the wastepaper basket lay on its side; and his lips tightened when he saw the open lid of his bureau. The lock hung from a jagged splinter of wood. The small drawers inside were askew. An urgent moment of searching told him that the wallet containing the diamonds was missing.

Over the 'phone he told his story to Victoria Lincoln, at her office in Kingward House, Regent Street.

' . . . Andrew Holmes here, Miss Lincoln . . . speaking from 71 Burlington Gardens. I've just returned from dining out to find my flat broken into and some very valuable diamonds missing from the bureau. Will you come round right away? Very good . . . I'll wait.'

He slotted the receiver back on its cradle, gave himself a cigarette. He made no attempt to straighten the room, but relaxed on the settee, smoking slowly, with his eyes half-closed. Some twenty minutes later his bell rang. He went to the door, opened it; a slim, dark-haired elegantly-dressed young lady stepped inside, followed by a girl with glossy blonde hair under a *chic* black beret.

Victoria Lincoln smiled sweetly, held out her hand in a sincere gesture.

'Pleased to meet you, Mr. Holmes! May I introduce my assistant — Miss Caroline Gerrard?'

Holmes shook hands with Victoria, then with Carol. He indicated the open door of his study.

'In here, ladies please. Nothing's been disturbed . . . '

After telling Carol to dust the room for fingerprints, Victoria's first question was:

'You said you'd been out dining, Mr. Holmes? What time did you leave your flat?'

'About six. I always go out to dine about that time. I returned, as usual, about seven-thirty.' He shrugged, indicated the mess the thief had left behind. 'This evening I came back to this . . . so I 'phoned you right away.'

'A splendid idea, Mr. Holmes!' Victoria murmured, with a smile. 'Now — can you think of anyone who'd *know* about your flat being empty . . . between six and seven-thirty?'

'Yes — Doctor Keith Wilson. He has the flat on the floor below. We usually dine out together — but this evening he excused himself, saying he had a patient to visit at Kingston — a Mrs. Esmond.'

'I see. D'you know much about him, Mr. Holmes? How long he's been in practice, and so on?'

'Six months or so, Miss Lincoln — that's all. This is his first attempt to start a practice. Between ourselves, of course, he's told me several times that he's desperately short of money. Often I've thought he's been paving the way for a request for a loan — but he's never suggested that as yet.'

'Well. That's useful, Mr. Holmes,' Miss Lincoln carefully smoothed a fresh page in her notebook. 'You know, just for interest — I'd like to find out whether Dr. Wilson *did* have an appointment with this special patient tonight. See — what was the name . . . Esmond, wasn't it?'

'That's right.' Holmes jumped up, went over to the table where the 'phone lay, came back with the book. 'Well, we can soon find out, Miss Lincoln — if you think it'll help.'

He sat down again, thumbing through the book.

'I know the name and address — we'll soon find the number . . . here it is . . . Esmond, Greylands . . . Kingston double-seven-five-seven . . . '

Carol had finished her dusting now. She came over to her boss, handed her a large envelope. An atmosphere of tenseness hung about the room as they watched Holmes go to the 'phone.

In a few moments he was through:

'Kingston double-seven-five-seven? Good. Well . . . I'm a friend of Dr. Wilson's . . . he told me he was coming out to your place tonight. Are you Mrs. Esmond? She's out . . . oh, I see, she's not been in this evening, at *any* time? You're sure? Right . . . thank you very much.'

He hung up, turned to Victoria.

'Well, that's it, Miss Lincoln! That was the maid speaking. Mrs. Esmond left for town about four-thirty this afternoon and hasn't returned yet. The maid doesn't expect her back until well after midnight, either — she's gone to a big dance at the Imperial.' He leaned both hands on the back of the settee. 'What's the next move?'

Miss Lincoln stood up slowly, pocketed her notebook and pencil.

'I think the next move is a talk with Dr. Wilson. Suppose you show us to his rooms, Mr. Holmes?'

Holmes nodded, went to the door, held it open.

'This way, ladies,' he said.

★   ★   ★

Victoria Lincoln, after one brief glance, thought that Dr. Wilson was a likeable, wholesome character.

Young, sunburned, with vital dark eyes

and black hair. He stood near the table now, looking perplexedly from one to the other. Holmes cleared his throat, nodded at Victoria.

'This is a private detective and her assistant, Doctor — Miss Victoria Lincoln . . . and Miss Carol Gerrard. My flat has been robbed, and we — I . . .'

He coughed again, and paused.

The doctor's brows wrinkled.

'*Robbed*, Andrew? Good heavens! Anything very valuable missing?'

Miss Lincoln said:

'Diamonds, Doctor. We came to see you because we think maybe you can help us.'

'Me?' Wilson's voice held a note of astonishment. 'How on earth can *I* help you?'

He laughed, a little shakily.

Miss Lincoln shrugged slightly.

'Hardly a matter for mirth, Doctor. Perhaps you'd care to tell us to whom you made your visit this evening?'

Wilson's face lost some of its colour.

'Well, of course — no objection at all to telling you where I've been. A Mrs.

Esmond, out at Kingston. I believe I told you, Andy, when I saw you at teatime.'

Holmes nodded. Victoria coughed, and then said:

'We 'phoned Mrs. Esmond a few minutes ago, Doctor. She wasn't in. Her maid told us she hadn't *been* in since four-thirty this afternoon and wasn't expected back until very late.'

She spoke slowly, watching Wilson's face closely for the slightest sign of consternation; but she looked in vain for the doctor nodded eagerly, and then spoke without hesitation.

'You didn't let me finish, Miss Lincoln. I was going to tell you that the call was a mistake. When I arrived at Mrs. Esmond's place her maid told me her mistress was perfectly well and had gone to town for the evening. She couldn't understand me getting the call — neither can I.'

Victoria said: 'I see, Doctor. Now, have you any objection to us searching your place?'

Dr. Wilson sat down abruptly. With Victoria's words, a grimness crept into the atmosphere and he was quick to sense it. He said curtly:

'Go ahead, madam. I've no objection.'

Holmes stood near the fireplace while Victoria and Carol set to work smoothly, efficiently. Ten minutes went by, crept to fifteen. They came back from the bedroom, shaking their heads. Miss Lincoln said:

'Nothing, Mr. Holmes — nothing at all.'

As Wilson rose to his feet Holmes said something in an undertone to the detective. They all moved away from the fireplace. In the hearth stood a small screen made of black glass with a motif of crimson flowers. Victoria bent, fiddled about at the back of it. A top section of the glass slid out. Wilson started forward as Miss Lincoln inserted her hand. When she straightened she held a small leather pouch. Carol moved close to Dr. Wilson as Victoria opened out the pouch onto the table.

Three large uncut diamonds slid out. They lay there glistening with a myriad flashing fires. Dr. Wilson started spluttering. Miss Lincoln looked at Holmes.

'Can you identify them, Mr. Holmes?'

Holmes spoke complacently.

'I can, miss. They're mine all right. And thank you for a *very* smart piece of work!'

The doctor found his voice,

'What *is* all this?' he shouted. 'Somebody planted those diamonds there! I didn't know . . . I — '

He broke off as Victoria Lincoln's voice cut at him.

'I'm sending for the police, Dr. Wilson. I'm charging you with the theft of these stones. Perhaps you'd prefer to come to the station without any fuss?'

Wilson's face was white now, his voice icy.

'All right, Miss Lincoln. I'll come along. But believe me, you're making a dreadful mistake!'

Holmes moved to the door. Carol followed quickly as they passed through.

* * *

Next afternoon the detective and Carol held a short conference in Victoria's private office.

Carol said: 'You're not satisfied with this case, are you, Vicky? Although everything points to Dr. Wilson being the thief — I know you're not satisfied. Am I right?'

' 'Fraid you are, my dear. Inside, I'm not convinced. Know what I mean? Instinct. Wilson isn't the *kind* of man, that's all — even if he *is* hard up, even if he is having a hard struggle to get on. But I just can't *see* him stealing diamonds. I'd as soon believe my own mother doing it. It just doesn't *fit* . . . '

She turned quickly as her secretary, Pam Wentworth, poked her head round the door.

'A Mr. Reginald Wilson to see you, Miss Lincoln. Very urgent, he says. Shall I — ?'

Miss Lincoln nodded.

'Show him in, please, Pamela.'

She placed another chair beside the desk. Mr. Wilson was shown in. Victoria indicated the chair.

'What can we do for you, Mr. Wilson?'

She studied the visitor keenly as Wilson sat down uneasily. She saw a tall, soldierly figure with iron-grey hair, and clipped moustache, a lined face and dark, heavy eyes. Victoria was accustomed to seeing people face to face with tremendous conflict. She leaned back, waiting for Wilson to speak.

'It's about my son, Miss Lincoln — Dr. Keith Wilson. This terrible business has made me into an old man overnight. I'm convinced beyond all vestige of doubt that an awful mistake has been made. I'm offering a reward of a thousand pounds to anyone who can clear my son's name. The case isn't closed, Miss Lincoln? Investigations are still proceeding?'

Victoria spread her slender hands. Carol coughed. Victoria said:

'Well, you know the facts, sir. Circumstantially, the case against your boy is watertight. I agree with you, wholeheartedly, that it's an extraordinary business. But what can we do?'

Something in the detective's tone gave Wilson the encouragement he needed. He leaned forward, his eyes glowing.

'Keep trying, Miss Lincoln! This is life or death to me and my boy. Tackle the case again, try a fresh approach. You'll find me *very* generous, I promise you. There must be something . . . *some* way . . . '

He bit his lips, which were trembling slightly.

Victoria jumped up, held out her hand. There was no point in prolonging this interview.

'Leave it to us, Mr. Wilson. I admit I'm not satisfied with the case, as a whole. You can rest assured that your boy will get a fair deal.'

Wilson nodded his thanks, but didn't trust himself to speak. When the door closed behind him Victoria Lincoln stared at Caroline.

'Now what?' she asked. 'The case is signed, sealed and delivered — but I can't let it rest. What can we do?'

Carol gazed through the window at the ever-streaming traffic if Regent Street.

'One thing sticks out, Vicky.' She spoke eagerly. 'Why did Dr. Wilson tell Holmes about his fake alibi? I mean the Esmond business. Why did he *tell* Holmes he was off to visit Mrs. Esmond particularly?

Why not just say he was going to visit a patient — any patient?'

Victoria said softly:

'Ah! A beautiful bit of reasoning, my dear! Your point is, that Wilson mentioned Mrs. Esmond because he really *believed* he was going there; because he believed that the 'phone call he had, really *came* from her place. Is that what you mean?'

'That's it, Vicky. The problem is: if Mrs. Esmond didn't phone, who did . . . and why?'

Victoria squared up to the desk, put her arms on it.

'Look . . . suppose someone wanted the doctor out of the way? Or ruined professionally. Doctors find out all sorts of things about all sorts of people, you know, Carol — and maybe Wilson knows too much about somebody and it's making them rather uncomfortable, All right — they decide to do something about it. First, they lure him from his flat, with a fake 'phone call from one of his patients. While he's gone, they plant the diamonds in his fire-screen. Then the robbery is staged, in Holmes' flat — and

Holmes calls me in, in the ordinary way.'

'You mean Holmes is — is working for whoever it is who wants Dr. Wilson out of the way?'

'Exactly. Here's another thing: it was Andrew Holmes *himself* who whispered to me to search the fire-screen. Yes . . . he said that once the Doctor had shown him the secret cavity in its glass top!'

Carol nodded slowly.

'Naturally . . . if they'd put the diamonds there, they weren't going to let us go until we'd found them!'

Miss Lincoln was on her feet.

'You know, I honestly think we're on the right track, my dear. I've a feeling I'd like to interview that Mrs. Esmond. How'd you like a ride out there?'

'That'd be grand, Vicky!' Carol said eagerly.

'All right. Grab your hat and let's go . . . '

★   ★   ★

Less than an hour later they were swishing up the wide, tree-lined driveway of Greylands.

A tall, immaculate woman answered their ring. She stared at them imperiously.

'I'm Mrs. Esmond. What is your business?'

Victoria Lincoln explained.

Mrs. Esmomd said:

'I'm afraid I cannot help you, young lady. I was in town all last evening. I returned about two this morning. When I came down for lunch today I found an empty house. My maid — Irene Chambers — had left suddenly, it seemed — her few things were still in her room. Then, about an hour ago, I had a 'phone call from some relation of hers. It seems one of her aunts or something has been taken ill and she's had to go at once to nurse her. The caller gave an address where I could send her things. It's really most annoying . . . I'm all alone here . . . '

Victoria tut-tutted sympathetically.

'And you've no idea how or why Dr. Wilson received your call?'

'Not the faintest. It certainly didn't come from me. What *is* all this about, d'you think? Is it anything very serious?'

Miss Lincoln said gravely:

'I expect Dr. Wilson thinks so, madam. You'd help us a lot if you could give us that address — the one where you're sending your maid's things.'

'Certainly.' She fumbled in her bag. 'Here — two-seventy-two, Fillmore Street, Battersea.'

Victoria made a note.

'Many thanks, Mrs. Esmond. We shan't have to trouble you any further.'

Across London they could only make slow progress. It was nearly five o'clock when they turned into Fillmore street. Number 272 was a little transport café.

'Where's the boss?' said Victoria, to an untidy youth busy serving teas and buns.

The patrons stopped eating and drinking to stare at such 'posh' visitors. The youth went red and then white.

'Maw!' he yelled. 'Two ladies want yer.'

He stood back and gaped, his customers forgotten.

Presently a stout, greasy woman ambled in from the back regions. She heard Miss Lincoln's story, then shook her head blankly.

'Can't 'elp yer, ladies! This 'ere is a

respectable café, yer can see that. 'Course, I ain't sayin' but what somebody may be *usin'* this address, see? But that ain't my fault, is it?'

She'd taken them through to her living room. Victoria said:

'All right, madam. Listen: Mrs. Esmond will be sending that parcel here, addressed to Miss Chambers. Now, I want you to keep it. See? Then if anyone calls for it, contact us immediately — and keep them here till we come. You'll do that?'

' 'Course I will, lady. All for law an' order, me. Well . . . I'm Mrs. Potts . . . Just tell me where to get 'old of yer. It'll be all right . . . '

Victoria's next move was to call at Bow Street Police Station. After a few moments they were shown into the office of her good friend Inspector Ralph Grayson.

Victoria said:

'This Wilson case promises to be quite exciting, Inspector!!

Grayson was red-faced, hearty, ponderous of movement.

'What's been happening?' he asked.

Victoria told him. The Inspector's

brows were creased, as he scratched his forehead.

'You seem to be attaching tremendous importance to this serving girl, don't you, Miss Victoria? What on earth has *she* to do with it — even supposing your suspicions of Holmes are correct?'

Victoria's dark brown eyes flashed as she leaned forward.

'Don't expect me to explain now, Inspector. I want to see first if I'm right. Look — will you trust me far enough to release Dr. Wilson?'

Caroline jumped then as Grayson's heavy fist banged the desk.

'Really, Miss Lincoln! You're asking *too* much! You — '

'Am I?' Victoria spoke softly. 'So sorry, Inspector. But I'm convinced that some-one wants the doctor out of the way — perhaps only for a while, or perhaps they want to stop him practising as a doctor, for some reason; and I'm convinced also that Holmes, and probably several more people, are mixed up in the plot.'

Her voice took on a pleading note.

Inwardly, Carol chuckled.

'So, surely, Inspector,' Victoria continued, 'the only way to force their hand, to bring them out into the open — is to free Wilson? They're bound to make another attempt on him when they know he's free — and they'll walk right into our trap. It'll be easy enough . . . all you need do is send the papers a story about new evidence coming to light, and that Wilson is being released, pending a fresh investigation. Trust me, Inspector! *Please* . . . '

'With Dr. Wilson out of jail,' said Caroline, 'I'm *certain* things will start happening, sir!'

Inspector Grayson shrugged. His heavy face broke into a smile.

'Oh, all right . . . with two lovely ladies pestering him, what's a poor policeman to do?'

Carol caught Victoria's eye and winked as Grayson reached for the 'phone.

★   ★   ★

The tall man in the black overcoat and dark Homburg hat looked up at the number on the door of the little café, 272, it said. He pushed the door open, went in, leant against the counter.

'Yes, mister?'

'Er — I've called for a parcel addressed to a Miss Chambers. Do you — ?'

'Chambers. 'Arf a minute.'

The youth disappeared into the rear of the shop. It was quite a while before he returned.

'Ma's 'avin' a look, mister,' he reported. 'She thinks one did come a few days ago, an' she put it in the storeroom, thinkin' someone'd be callin' for it. She'll be down in a minute. Like a cup of tea?'

'Thanks. I will.'

The stranger took his tea, sat down at a table, idly studied a newspaper. Ten minutes went by before Victoria Lincoln's car drew into the kerb outside.

She entered the café, Carol at her heels, and went quickly to the table where the stranger sat. He leapt to his feet when he saw who it was.

Victoria said:

'All right, Dr. Keith Wilson! I think this just about settles things, doesn't it? You were afraid that if the parcel was left here too long questions might be asked about it, and the strange disappearance of the maid would be discovered!'

Wilson was on his feet, his eyes blazing.

'Just what *is* all this, Miss Lincoln? Be very careful — '

Victoria cut in:

'You murdered Miss Chambers so that there'd be no one who could swear you hadn't been at the Esmond's at the time of the robbery! You had her things sent here so that Mrs. Esmond wouldn't get suspicious when her maid didn't return. Why *here?* Because you'd probably noticed the place on your rounds and realized it was as good as any for an accommodation address. Am I right, Doctor?'

Wilson's face was white, his tone icy.

'You're crazy, madam! Someone 'phoned me at the flat, saying if I called here and asked for a parcel addressed to a Miss Chambers, I'd find valuable evidence that would prove my innocence. The call came at a few minutes past four. They'll have a record of it in the reception office at Burlington Gardens — maybe we can find out where it was sent from . . .'

Miss Lincoln looked hard at the doctor.

'Perhaps I'm an awful fool — but I believe you!' she said with a smile. 'In that case, Doctor, Carol, we'll go to Burlington Gardens, and see if we can trace that call.'

Yes . . . the telephonist in the block of flats had a record of the call.

'Four minutes after four, ma'am,' she told the detective.

'Any idea from whom?' Victoria asked.

'No, ma'am. The caller just said to give the message to Dr. Wilson.'

'There you are!' Wilson said, triumphantly. 'What did I tell you?'

Victoria's keen eyes were gleaming now. She turned to Carol and the doctor.

'Back to Bow Street, you people. We'll contact the Exchange from there, and trace that call.

Half an hour later the three were sitting in Grayson's office when a clerk came in with a slip of paper, which he handed to Grayson. The Inspector tapped it with his pencil.

'Well, here it is, folks. Doctor, your mysterious caller 'phoned from Brixton Double-two-double-two. Any use?'

Doctor Wilson had jumped up.

'Any use? By God, I'll say it is! Four twos, and Brixton — I remember *that* number all right! I — I — '

He spluttered. Grayson waved him into his chair.

'Sit down, Doctor — take it easy. Just tell us what you know.'

Wilson sat down, gripped the arms of the chair.

'Listen, you people. It was on Easter Monday. There was a car accident in Berkeley Square, and as I was passing at the time I rendered first aid to one passenger who'd broken an arm. While I was attending to him I discovered that he was a marvellous case of heterotaxy! He gave me five pounds for my trouble and I couldn't think of any reason for asking for his name and address, although I was deeply interested in his condition.'

Inspector Grayson grunted.

'Heterotaxy? What the dickens is that?'

'A very rare condition, Inspector — his

heart was on the wrong side of his chest. Anyway, I was so curious that when his car drove away eventually, I took his number, meaning to think of some excuse to look him up later. I traced the number, but it was a hired car. Yes, gentleman — hired from a Brixton garage number double-two-double-two. I called there once or twice but they refused to tell me who'd hired the car on that day. So I let the matter drop.'

Ralph Grayson was on his feet now, rummaging in a filing cabinet.

'There you are, Miss Lincoln! Isaac Klepstein's dossier. He escaped from Wandsworth last Easter Monday and he's still at large!'

Victoria stroked her chin, with pale slender fingers.

'Doctor — maybe you attended to a very notorious bank robber that day! Maybe that explains quite a few things!'

There was a moment's silence, then she smacked the desk with her fist.

'Great Scott!' she said. She spoke through tightened lips. 'Folks — I'm beginning to see the light! Our next flying visit is to that garage in Brixton. And *this* time, Doctor, believe *me* — those people will talk!'

* * *

A fortnight later the strange case of the young doctor was finally closed. Klepstein was back in jail, and Holmes had confessed to the murder of Miss Chambers; also he'd admitted to being with Klepstein, in the Bond Street Bank robbery.

In Grayson's office sat the inspector, Victoria Lincoln and Caroline, going over the final details.

'A vicious little gang, by all accounts,' Victoria Lincoln said, gravely. 'It was Dr. Wilson's interest in Klepstein's heterotaxy that set the ball rolling. For when Wilson kept calling at the garage, which the gang used as a hideout and headquarters, naturally they became suspicious. Klepstein would think: 'Ah, the doctor has discovered my condition, made a few enquiries, and has found out that I'm an escaped convict. We'll have him out of the way, quick!

'Because Klepstein knew that the strange condition of his heart would eventually give him away as the bank robber, if the doctor kept on being so inquisitive. So he sends Holmes to live in the next flat to Dr. Wilson, to make friends and so on — and presto! The jewel robbery was all staged very nicely, as we saw.

'Now, to complete the scheme, they had to set the law on Dr. Wilson. Naturally, Holmes, being a crook, was scared to contact the police direct. Hence his 'phone call to me.

'You might ask: Why didn't they kill Wilson? Well, my guess is that they wanted a doctor for the gang, and for Klepstein especially, considering his state. Who better than Wilson, after his release from jail? He'd have been ruined and would have jumped at any offer. *And* he'd have kept quiet.

'As for the unfortunate Miss Chambers — well, they realized *she* could have established an alibi for the doctor. She'd have said, when questioned: 'Yes, Dr.

Wilson is telling the truth. He *did* call here about six-thirty on that particular night, but Mrs. Esmond was out.

'So later, on the night of the robbery, Holmes calls at Greylands, and when she answers the door, shoots her through the head, and throws her body in the lily pond. Then, so that Mrs. Esmond wouldn't get suspicious, they made up that tale about one of her relations being ill, and asked for her clothes to be sent to the café in Fillmore Street. Mrs. Potts, by the way, is quite innocent of any connection with the gang.

'Now, when they read in the papers that Dr. Wilson had been released, they realized something had gone wrong with their schemes. They guessed, no doubt, that we'd be watching the café to see who claimed the parcel. Hence the false 'phone call to the doctor about it containing valuable evidence that would prove his innocence. As before, he walked right into their trap!'

Inspector Grayson nodded slowly.

'A really nasty, vicious little crew, eh, Miss Victoria? But they didn't show much fight when we raided their garage!'

Victoria Lincoln smiled and Carol said:

'Well, you didn't give them much time to think, did you, Inspector? Much less to defend themselves!'

6

TRAP FOR A KILLER

Sergeant Harry Kirtlan was on duty in the charge room at Kilburn Police Station when Victoria Lincoln walked in — followed by Caroline Gerrard.

'Good morning, Sergeant!' Victoria said cheerfully.

'Ah, good morning, Miss Lincoln!' The burly sergeant indicated Carol. 'Who's the young lady?'

Victoria's white teeth flashed in a sudden smile.

'Meet my assistant, Sergeant — Miss Caroline Gerrard. She left college only a few month's ago . . . but she's beginning to teach me a few tricks already!'

They all laughed as Carol and Sergeant Kirtlan shook hands.

'What brings you down to our little corner of the globe, ladies?'

'The Piper case, Sergeant. A friend of the dead man has asked me to look into things. Can you help us at all?'

Kirtlan shrugged his heavy shoulders.

'A plain case of suicide, Miss Lincoln. Arranged himself on the sofa on some cushions, then put a bullet right through his own heart. His clothing was scorched all round the wound, the gun was on the floor by his right hand. Money was his trouble it seems . . . and he'd quarrelled with his wife. There was a note in his breast pocket.'

He handed over a grubby document.

'That's it, Miss Lincoln.'

Victoria beckoned to her assistant. As she read, Caroline looked over her shoulder.

Dear Wife,

I know I have not been a good husband, but never mind, all is over now and I am leaving for good. I cannot raise a cent and no hopes of a job, so I am best out of the way. Good luck, my love.

Your loving husband,

Fred.

Victoria Lincoln nodded, folded the

note, laid it on the desk.

'It's his writing all right, I suppose? Who identified it?'

'Eh? The writing? Oh, yes . . . his missus says it's his, right enough.'

'I see. Anything else, Sergeant?'

'Look — there's nothing to worry about, Miss Lincoln. From the line the bullet took and the way the clothing is burned around the hole — the gun was pressing on his chest when it was fired . . . that's certain. I'd say a cast-iron certainty. Then there's the note he left, and all that. Pretty straight case, I imagine.'

'Well . . . you're probably right. Any marks on the body at all?'

Kirtlan scratched his massive chin before he answered. Then, with a slight gesture of impatience:

'There was a slight bruise, Miss Lincoln . . . left side of the chin; but it's nothing. I — '

'Ah! A bruise? Made, then, a very short time before he died?'

'Well . . . Yes, I'd say so. Bumped it somewhere, I expect.'

'I see. Well, thanks very much, Sergeant. I hope we'll be able to help *you* some day!'

She beckoned to Carol, who followed her out.

They went back past the station on the High Road. Ten minutes' sharp walking in the direction of Kilburn brought them to Albany Street — a long line of dun-coloured houses with their front doors opening on to the pavement. They found No. 29, and rang the bell. A pale-faced little woman presently opened the door. She had a round elfin face and a stubby nose that struck Carol as being absurdly comical. Wisps of faded brown hair straggled down her cheeks. Miss Lincoln smiled and showed her card. The woman's hands fluttered to her mouth.

'Oh, dear . . . you're a detective? Oh . . . well, come in ma'am . . . this dreadful business, I'm sure . . . I don't know . . .'

She took them into the front room, stood nervously facing them across the table.

'Mrs. Piper, I'd like your version of this unfortunate affair. Just for my own

222

records, you understand,' Victoria Lincoln said, quietly.

'Y-e-s . . . well, I went out shopping yesterday evening . . . every Friday night I go, about six . . . a few things for the weekend, you know. Fred was all right when I left — quite all right . . . he was sitting in the kitchen reading the newspaper. Then when I got back about seven — there he was lying on the sofa . . . dead. Poor feller! But I'm worse off without him, ma'am . . . it's that lonely and quiet . . . I can't stand it . . . '

She pulled out a handkerchief, started dabbing her eyes.

Victoria waited. In a moment she mentioned the bruise. Had Mrs. Piper any idea at all how Frederick came by it? A fall, perhaps . . . or had he bumped into anything recently?

'No ma'am — can't say I remember him doing anything. A bruise on his chin?' She shook her head several times. Miss Lincoln watched her closely. ''Course, I wasn't with him *all* day and night . . . if he'd had a bump he didn't mention nothing to me.'

'I see. Now this letter he left, Mrs. Piper. You're quite sure it was his writing?'

She set her mouth primly.

'Why certainly. 'Dear Lily,' he said, 'I know I haven't been a good husband to you . . . ' There . . . you see? Folks tell you I've had a hard struggle to keep going, ma'am . . . this last two years Fred never did a stroke of work. Aye, he wrote it all right. I can't see nobody else putting such as *that* in a letter except my own husband!'

Miss Lincoln tried another angle.

'Could you show me another letter of his, Mrs. Piper? Or something he'd written sometime . . . just to compare them, you see? To make quite sure . . . '

' 'Fraid I can't, Miss Lincoln. Fred never wrote *me* a letter in his life. And really I can't ever remember seeing him with a pen in his hand — nor a pencil, far as that goes. Fred was only a labourer, ma'am. His money wasn't big even when he was working. Why, many's the week he — '

Victoria raised her hand.

'I see your point, Mrs. Piper. Now one

thing more. When you went out last evening did you lock the place up?'

'Yes. But the back door would have been open . . .'

'I see. There's a back way in?'

'Yes. There's a lane running at the backs of these houses. Our door in the wall is never locked either. Tell you the truth, there isn't a lock on it.'

'So . . . through your back garden . . . that'd be an easy way for a visitor to come and go, Mrs. Piper . . . unseen by anyone . . . eh?'

'Why, Ma'am!' Again her thin hands twitched at her mouth. 'Lawks! Surely you don't think Poor Fred was — was *murdered*?' Her eyes, now wide and staring, gaped at the detective incredulously.

Victoria stood up.

'No, no, Mrs. Piper — I didn't say that. I tell you, I'm just curious about that bruise. But maybe it was nothing — nothing at all.'

They moved to the door. She followed them out, held the front door open.

'Good day, Mrs. Piper. Do try and keep cheerful — don't make yourself ill through it. Will you?'

Mrs. Piper nodded, her lips all bunched up in her puckered little face. Miss Lincoln saluted gravely as she and Carol walked off down the street.

★ ★ ★

Back on the main road again, Victoria indicated a stall across the street. They went over. As they sipped coffee Caroline asked quietly:

'Found any clues yet, Vicky?'

Victoria smiled.

'Sometimes I wish I *was* a miracle-worker, Carol — for your sake! No . . . the only thing in this case that's in any way peculiar is that bruise on Mr. Pipers' chin. I'd like to find out about that.'

'You think Mrs. Piper might have given it to him? Well . . . why not make enquiries in the street — amongst the neighbours? *They'd* know if the Pipers were good friends or not.'

Miss Lincoln squeezed her young assistant's arm affectionately.

'That's just why we're killing time here,

my dear! I didn't like to call next door with Mrs. Piper in her doorway . . . '

Carol grinned, nodding quickly.

'I see, Vicky. Sorry . . . '

They finished their coffee, went slowly back down Albany Street, stopping this time at No. 27. A plump, grey-haired female answered their knock. Victoria smiled pleasantly, presented her card.

'Just a few routine enquiries into the sad death next door . . . Mr. Piper. May we come in?'

Again the front room with its shiny furniture and unused appearance. Miss Lincoln said:

'You realise, about them. We'd be glad to hear it, madam — as the Pipers' neighbour . . . if you know of anything unusual about them, we'd be glad to hear it. There's nothing wrong, you understand — nothing at all; but on these occasions we always . . . you know?'

She elevated her eyebrows, closed one eye discreetly. Then:

'Now . . . your name, please?'

'Jesmond — yes — Mrs. Jesmond.'

'And to the best of your knowledge and

belief the Pipers were a friendly couple? You never heard then quarrelling — I mean really seriously.'

'Why, no. Can't say I ever have, ma'am.'

'Hmm. Were you on friendly terms with the Pipers, Mrs. Jesmond? You knew them well?'

'Fairly. I used to slip in and read the paper to Mrs. Piper of an evening sometimes, when Fred was out at the club. She couldn't read a word, you know. Yes, it's true — not a word.'

There was a pause. Miss Lincoln felt the thrill of a hunter on the first spoor of the quarry.

'I see. That's very interesting, Mrs. Jesmond. Now, consider last evening, between six and seven. To the best of your knowledge no one called on the Pipers during that time? If so, I thought maybe you might've seen them, coming or going through the back lane.'

She shook her head. 'I saw no one, ma'am. Mind, I wasn't watching out, so that's nothing to go by.'

'No — I see, well, many thanks, Mrs.

Jesmond. I don't think we need bother you any further.'

She let them out. Again they walked to the main road, drank more coffee. Victoria said softly:

'So dear Mrs. Piper can't read a word, eh, Carol? I don't see how she could identify her husband's writing, then . . . '

'Another point, Vicky — she said the note began with 'Dear Lily' . . . but you read it as 'Dear wife'!'

'So I did, Carol — so I did. Mrs. Piper either knew about that note beforehand — or else someone read it to her and she's forgotten the exact words. Tell you what . . . we'll make *another* call in Albany Street — this time at the house on the other side — Number 31.'

They finished their coffee, went back to Albany Street. This time they went round the back lane, through the wall gate of No. 31. In an outhouse a woman in damp, dirty overalls was putting clothes through a mangle. The detective explained her business.

The woman screwed up her eyes, thought deeply.

'Last night, ma'am? Let's see — between six and seven . . . huh . . . I was out at the pictures. But my Jimmy was in. We left him looking after the baby.'

She turned towards the house, raised her voice.

'Jimmy! Come out here for a moment. Lady wants to speak to you.'

A youngster of about twelve came out biting at a slice of bread-and-jam.

'Jimmy — this lady says was there anybody called at the Pipers' last night, while me and your Dad was out?'

Jimmy thought for a moment, going as red as a beetroot.

'Yeah, mum — there was . . . a good bit after you'd gone. I kicked my ball over into the Pipers' yard. I went round and rang the bell but there was no answer. So I nipped over the wall . . . and I saw a man running up the path and he went out the back gate.'

'Did you get a good look at him, sonny?' Miss Lincoln asked.

'Well, no — I didn't actually. I never bothered much. But I think he had red hair. He had a cap on, but it was kind of long on his neck. I'm almost sure he had red hair.'

'Well, thanks a lot, sonny,' said Victoria. 'You've been very useful. Can you give me any idea about what time this would be?'

'See — I'd been listening to the football talk after the six o'clock news . . . I'd just switched off and gone into the yard . . . reckon it'd be about half past six, lady.'

'Right. Thank you. Well, good afternoon, sonny. Good afternoon, madam. Come on, Carol.'

Back in the little lane the detective paused.

'Carol, what was the address of the doctor who was called in after Fred Piper was found shot?'

Carol opened the brief case, glanced at the Piper notes.

'Doctor de Fraine — Osmond House, Oakland Street.'

'Right! I'd like a talk with him before we go.'

They found him two streets away, behind a shiny brass plate on a small, drab house; a neatly dressed, elderly gentlemen with thin, greying hair and a lined, wise face. He bowed politely as Victoria did the introductions and explained their business.

'Just what can I do for you, ladies?'

'You were called to the Piper home last night, doctor?'

'I was. 'Fraid there's not much I can tell you. He was quite dead when I arrived there. Bullet wound was through his waistcoat and underclothes. Suicide all right, I haven't a doubt. Look: he had a cigarette case in his inside breast pocket, covering his heart. It was like that when I went to him. I had to move the jacket to feel for his heart. You see? The weight of the case had caused the jacket to flop back over the wound, *after* the pistol fell away. If anyone else had shot him the bullet would've went through the case. Am I right, Miss Lincoln?'

'It seems like it, Doctor. I take it you searched the body, then?'

'No, no — I left that to the police. I merely felt inside his breast pocket and found just the case there.'

'Nothing else?'

'Nothing else at all.'

Miss Lincoln jumped up.

'Very well, Doctor. Thanks for your assistance. We won't detain you any further.'

Outside, she hailed a taxi. As they bundled in, she said to the driver:

'Kilburn Police Station, please.' Then, grimly, to her youthful assistant: 'I want another chat with Sergeant Kirtlan in double quick time, Carol!'

* * *

Kirtlan tapped impatiently on the desk with his fingertips. He hadn't expected Victoria to come back.

'Yes, Miss Lincoln? Anything wrong?'

'H'mm . . . 'fraid you've handled this case rather slackly, Sergeant. Why didn't you tell me Mrs. Piper never read that note her husband left?'

'Eh? She never read . . . ? Oh. I see. I — '

'Now suppose you say just what happened?'

233

'Well, Miss — naturally I handed her the note. She looked at it, screwed her eyes up, said she couldn't read a word without her glasses, and she'd broken 'em the day before. So I read it out to her. But she recognised her old man's writing. Everything was in order, Miss Lincoln.'

'That's what *you* think! All that nonsense was merely vanity on Mrs. Piper's part. She can't read a word, Sergeant . . . only she didn't like admitting it to you. Which means we've no proof whatever that Piper wrote that note at all. She said that she had nothing in the house with his writing — so unless we can find something, how are we to compare?'

Kirtlan scratched his bulging chin. 'I see your point. It's a bit perplexing. What d'you suggest?'

'I have a few ideas, Sergeant. One more point: tell me exactly where the body was when you searched it. You must have searched it, because you found the note. Where did you do the job? At the house, in the ambulance, at the mortuary . . . or where?'

'Well, Miss, to tell you the truth . . .

Mrs. Piper was carrying on so, I didn't bother at the house. All I wanted was to get away; she kept getting hysterical, and throwing herself about. So I hustled out quick and took Piper down to the mortuary. I searched him there.'

'I see. Now think carefully, Sergeant. You say you found the note in the inside breast pocket. Was there a cigarette case there, too?'

'Yes, Miss.'

Kirtlan thought fleetingly what a changed person Victoria Lincoln was now she had her nose on the scent. No longer easy-going, pleasant . . . but vital, alive, vicious even. Her eyes glinted, her lips curled; her whole body fairly quivered with intense eagerness.

She went on:

'Right. Now, then: Dr. de Fraine says *he* felt inside that breast pocket, at the house — and there was nothing there, only the cigarette case. You get that? He was absolutely positive about it. Therefore the note was put there *after* you left the house. You agree, Sergeant?'

He nodded slowly.

Victoria continued:

'I suppose you took it back from the mortuary to Albany Street, and showed it to Mrs. Piper?'

'I did, Miss. Yes . . . '

'All right. Now think *very* carefully, Sergeant. Who could have touched the body, unseen by you . . . between you leaving the house and making the search?'

'Why, nobody . . . nobody at all. I was with it the whole time, Miss Lincoln!'

'Every minute? Every *second*, Sergeant? Consider . . . it takes seconds only to slip a note in a pocket. Now we'll suppose Piper *was* murdered. His killer intends to leave a note, but for some reason doesn't do so, at the house. Maybe he was disturbed, maybe he left it behind, maybe he thought of it *after* he'd committed the crime. The solid fact remains: he had the opportunity to plant that note on the body before you searched it. Also, he must have known you hadn't searched it, see? The body is there, so is he. And you're out of the way for a moment, or looking elsewhere or something — and he thinks: 'Right, now's my chance, here goes . . . ' and he pops the note in!'

Kirtlan's fingers made a loud rasping sound on his chin. His face flushed darkly as he laboured to concentrate. It was obvious Miss Lincoln was on to something there. She leaned forward over the desk and said:

'Start at the house, Sergeant . . . Try and go over every move you made until you actually put your fingers inside that pocket and found that note.'

'All right, Miss.'

He leaned back, stared at the ceiling, his eyes puckered.

'I went to the house, saw the body, the gun, the burnt clothing. Ah, suicide plain enough, I reckoned. Then Mrs. Piper began her performance . . . I shoved the body out to the ambulance, took it to the mortuary, had it taken in. I told Hobson — that's the mortuary assistant, to stick it on the table, as I wanted to go through the pockets.'

'Ah. There's *one* man who knew you hadn't searched it! See what I mean, Sergeant?'

'I do indeed, Miss Lincoln. We got him on the table, then Hobson said, 'Just a minute, sir, that sounds like the 'phone.' You know — at the mortuary, the 'phone's in the front office, Miss. So Hobson goes through to answer it.'

'Knowing you wouldn't begin the search till he returned . . . he knows the procedure.'

'Well, yes — there's supposed to be another party present . . . anyhow, he comes back in a minute, says the call is for me. So I slips through, and — '

Victoria banged the desk, her face lighting up like a full moon.

'Hah! You see, for goodness sake . . . you *did* leave the body! Carry on, Sergeant . . . this is getting most interesting!'

'Seems to be, Miss! Well, the line seemed dead when I picked the receiver up. I kept yelling 'Hello' but nobody answered. So I hung up and went back. I asked Hobson who it was ringing, but he said the chap gave no name, just asked for me. Naturally I thought it was somebody from here, as they knew where I'd gone.

Well . . . we carried on then, going through Piper's pockets.'

'Things are adding up, Sergeant!' Miss Lincoln relaxed a little. 'Look — that 'phone call . . . did you actually *hear* it ringing, when Hobson said 'That sounds like the 'phone'?'

Kirtlan considered this point a moment.

'Can't say I did, at all. I never gave it a thought. Hobson just cocked his head on one side and listened, then popped off. No, Miss, now I come to think — *I* never heard it.'

'Well, then — couldn't it have been a ruse to get you away for a few minutes . . . long enough for him to plant the note?'

'*Hobson*? What on earth — why Hobson? Him, a murderer? It doesn't make sense, Miss Lincoln!'

'Maybe not; but he's the only man who *could* have put the note there, Sergeant. Providing, of course, that De Fraine made no mistake; and I'm inclined to think very firmly that he didn't. Still — Hobson hasn't red hair . . . '

'Red hair, Miss? What's that to do with it?'

'Well, you see, around six-thirty last evening, Mr. Piper had a visitor. A visitor who used the back way and who, according to the youth next door, had red hair that stuck out under his cap. Anyhow — what time does friend Hobson leave work? What are his hours?'

'Nine till six, Miss; and from the mortuary to Albany Street is only ten minutes sharp walking. Hobson's hair certainly isn't red though!'

'No — but he could've obtained some. A bit far-fetched, eh, Sergeant? All right, perhaps it is. We're dealing with a very crafty person here. If, of course, we have our hands on the right one! And if that 'phone call was a trick — well, Hobson's also clever enough to have placed a wig on his head when he slipped along to Albany Street, just in case a neighbour chanced to look through a window. He'd keep to the back lanes all along, and with his cap on, nobody would notice the false hair in the street. So it doesn't seem so silly after all. What's your opinion?'

Kirtlan was enthusiastic.

'By Jove, Miss Lincoln — you may well

be right! Now I come to think. Hobson's keen on theatricals. He does a bit with the Kilburn Amateur Dramatics — my lad's a member too. Well, there y'are — he could've pinched one of their wigs — eh?'

'So he could, Sergeant. Then there's that note. If Hobson wrote it, no doubt he'd disguise his hand. Now look — here's how I see it. Something tells me Piper didn't kill himself. There're too many funny points cropping up. That bruise on his chin, for one thing. What caused that? Why, the killer hit him, of course, and knocked him unconscious. See? So that he could get near enough to jab the gun right on his chest before he fired, to make it look like suicide. Anyhow . . . I'm slipping back for a chat with Hobson. Come on, Carol.'

Kirtlan jumped up, too.

'I'll come along, Miss, if I may?'

* * *

They found Hobson at his desk, adding up a row of figures in a ledger. Miss Lincoln went straight to the point.

'Hobson, we're not entirely satisfied that the Piper case is suicide. For one thing, the note he left behind was put in his pocket *after* the body left the house — and also there's no one who can positively swear it's in his writing. Now, you were the only man alone with the body before it was searched.'

She raised her hand when Hobson began to expostulate.

'Yes, I know — Sergeant Kirtlan was called to the 'phone and he left you alone with it then. Remember?'

Kirtlan said:

'Who was it called, Harry? Damned funny business that. The line was dead when *I* got to it.'

Hobson's thin face had paled. He'd put down his pen to hide the twitching of his hand, a movement that had not escaped Victoria Lincoln. She saw in Hobson, a hard-bitten type who'd no doubt endured a wearying life of constant bitter struggle. It showed in his protruding chin, in his tight, meagre lips, in the whole grim determination of his face.

Hobson said quietly:

242

'That 'phone call is a puzzle to me, too, Miss Lincoln. All I know is, somebody asked for Sergeant Kirtlan. I naturally supposed it was somebody from the police station.'

He didn't look at his callers, but kept his eyes on his ledger, only glancing up occasionally.

'Last night, Mr. Hobson . . . you went straight home from here? D'you live far away?' Victoria Lincoln asked.

'No — Fortune Green Road. Yes, I went right on home after I'd done a bit of shopping. I got back about six-thirty. I have a room there, Miss — just the one room. I get all my meals out.'

'I see.' Miss Lincoln glanced at Carol. 'Now, Mr. Hobson, just for a routine check, let me have a sample of your writing, please. Just a few lines, any words you like. Here, write on this.'

She placed her notebook on the desk in front of Hobson, who flushed a little and obliged without comment.

Victoria put the book away.

'One other point, Mr. Hobson — were you acquainted with the Pipers? Had you ever called there, at their home?'

'No, Miss Lincoln. First time I saw Piper was when Sergeant brought him in here.'

'All right. Thanks for the help. I don't think we need bother you further.'

Outside, Kirtlan said:

'Now what? Let's have a look at that writing, Miss Lincoln. Does it help at all?'

They stood in a shop doorway, looking at the letter and at what Hobson had written in the detective's notebook. The two hands were not very helpful to Victoria; either one or both could have been disguised. With a shrug and an exclamation of impatience Victoria put them away.

'Look, Sergeant — that's all for now. We're slipping back to the Yard to make a few enquiries. You'll be hearing from us later. So, cheerio for now!'

Miss Lincoln hailed a passing taxi. She and Carol were gone before Kirtlan could think of anything more to say.

★ ★ ★

They spent an instructive half-hour in the filing room at Scotland Yard. There they found a dossier, complete with photograph and fingerprints, of one Henry Melville Hobson, who, it appeared, had been convicted on May 11th, 1937, at Camberwell Police Court on a charge of bag-snatching. The chief witness against him had been Frederick Piper, of 29 Albany Street, NW9.

Later that afternoon Miss Lincoln and her assistant sat in a Whitehall tea shop, thoughtfully sipping tea.

Victoria said softly:

'Supposing Piper had been blackmailing Hobson, Carol? Suppose he'd told him: 'Either pay up or I tell your employer of your record and you lose a good job. And I'll follow wherever you go. I'll never let you rest'. Supposing he'd said that, Carol?'

'And — and Hobson killed him to keep him quiet?'

Victoria Lincoln smiled grimly.

'Murder has been done for less, my dear!'

★ ★ ★

The following evening, at a few minutes
past seven, Mr. H. H. Hobson had a
visitor at his apartments in Fortune
Green Road. The landlady called up the
stairs and he came down rubbing his
eyes, for he'd been dozing before the fire.
In the hall stood a slim, young-looking
man who sported a small moustache. He
wore a rather grubby raincoat and a big
black cap, which covered all his hair and
shaded his eyes at the same time.

Hobson said:

'Yes, young man? What can I do for
you?' He thought maybe he was a
debt-collector. He couldn't recollect ever
seeing him before.

'I'd like a word with you in private, Mr.
Hobson. It's rather a serious matter.'

On the way upstairs Hobson felt his
heart beating a little faster. When he'd
shut the door, he took a deep breath. He
sat at the table, waved his visitor to the
chair opposite. The man took a little card
from his pocket, handed it over.

Hobson read:

Acme Window Cleaning Co.
Contracts for Paint and
General Cleaning a Speciality.

Hobson, looking thoughtful, said:
'Well, lad, I'm afraid I can't do anything for you. The landlady sees to all that business. I just rent this room — you understand?' The caller smiled slightly.

'That's all right, Mr. Hobson. All I wanted to say was that a couple of days ago I was working Albany Street. About half past six or so I was doing the backs at No.29. There's a wash-house in the yard and I slipped in to swill my leathers out and get fresh water. When I came out I could see Mr. Piper had a visitor — a red-haired fellow who punched old Piper under the chin, laid him on the sofa, then pulled out a gun and shot him clean through the heart.

'See? And I followed that fellow back here, Mr. Hobson, and in a certain little place where nobody was looking, he pulled off his red hair and stuck it in a pocket. I had a little chat with your landlady this morning, and she told me what you looked like; so this evening I came along and asked for Mr. Hobson — and it's you all right!'

There was a long silence. Hobson's face went a dull red, but now it was deathly white. Under the table he gripped his knees to stop them shaking. He didn't trust himself to speak. He sat there staring at the table.

The man stroked his moustache and went on:

'Now look here, sir — I don't want to be awkward over this. Maybe you had a good reason for doing what you did — I'm not arguing with you about right and wrong. All I want is a hundred pounds and I'll keep quiet. Otherwise, I'm off to the police — right away. Is that clear?'

Mr. Hobson seemed to catch on; for after a while fifty pounds changed hands, which Hobson paid over in notes.

The man stood up then, twirled his moustache nonchalantly.

'You'll be seeing me again,' he said, before he shut the door.

★ ★ ★

An hour later the young man, whose name, you may have guessed, was Carol Gerrard, sat in Victoria Lincoln's office. On the desk between them lay the fifty pounds. Carol's deep blue eyes glinted as she looked at it.

'It worked, Vicky!' she said. 'What's the next move?'

Victoria smiled, gathered up the money.

'Proof positive, eh, Carol? Why, I'll ask the Public Prosecutor now to have Mr. Hobson arrested. I don't think he'll be a very hard nut to crack!'

Carol's eyes were glinting as she leaned forward.

'He's cracked wide open *now*, Vicky! Get after him while he's still trembling . . . '

7

TOO MANY CULPRITS

Victoria Lincoln, the famous detective, glanced up as Caroline Gerrard entered the office. Carol placed a box of confectionery on the desk as she handed her employer a typewritten note.

'The report says there was strychnine in the chocolate creams, Vicky. I remember you saying they were Mrs. Nixon's favourite, too! Mr. Nixon is signing a confession now . . . Inspector Grayson has just been on the 'phone.'

Victoria nodded.

'Sit down, my dear. This case has been simple — only one man *could* have done it. For contrast, I've just been looking up the Anderson files. Now *there* was something entirely different — a case of too many suspects!'

Carol looked up eagerly, all attention. Occasionally, when they had an odd hour to spare — and, as Victoria put it, 'as an important part of your training, my dear', she'd tell Carol about some particularly interesting case in which she'd been engaged earlier in her amazing career. Carol, recognising the symptoms now, realized that *this* was going to be one of those interesting occasions . . .

As the ebony-and-gold electric wall clock began softly to chime the hour of four, the door opened and Pamela Wentworth, Miss Lincoln's secretary, came in with the tea tray. Caroline poured out two cups, placed the biscuits within easy reach of both Victoria and herself, leaned back and crossed her legs.

Carol sipped her tea and waited expectantly.

★　★　★

One afternoon last July, Victoria commenced, I was called to Ashleigh manor, a few miles this side of Guildford. Sir George Anderson had been found dead in his rose garden; cause of death, apparently, plain heart failure. I took a police doctor along and as soon as he saw Anderson's face, with the mouth open

and contorted, he said: 'Tetanus poisoning' right away. Lockjaw, in other words,
Carol — germs of which can only enter
the body through a deep cut or a deep
needle prick.

We looked in vain for cuts or abrasions;
but in the fleshy pit of the thumb in the
right hand we found three punctures. We
decided there and then that the baronet's
death hadn't been just an accident. Was it
murder? In a peaceful country home, seat
of one of the oldest Surrey families? It
didn't seem possible . . .

First we made sure as to who'd come
and gone during the day. Beyond the
usual trades people, there'd been no
visitors. Sir George, a confirmed bach-
elor, had, since his retirement, lived a very
quiet life; the household comprised the
gardener — who'd found the body — the
housekeeper, the butler, and a young
protégé of Sir George's, who'd been with
the baronet since childhood, and who was
now regarded more as a son than
anything else.

Anyway, we began with the gardener,
Silas Andrews. His tale was that he'd

been at work on the marrow beds next to the rose garden; that, after lunch, Sir George went into the rose garden and for a while — about half an hour, Andrews reckoned — he could be heard busily snipping at his rose trees. Then Andrews moved out of earshot, but about an hour later had occasion to seek Sir George's advice. So he came back towards the marrow beds and looked around for his master.

Next minute he was running round the tall hedge surrounding the rose garden. At the far end lay Sir George, sprawled on the gravel pathway. He was dead by the time Andrews had fetched the butler to the scene.

The butler — Harlow, I think his name was — was the one who'd put through the call to me. I thought this was peculiar, and I told him so.

'Why send for *me*, Harlow? Do you *suspect* foul play?'

He wouldn't commit himself. He was tall and angular, with the frostiest blue eyes I've ever seen. He stared straight at me, never wavering.

'Can't say I do, Miss Lincoln. Don't know what made me send for you, particularly. I just thought it was the best thing to do. Especially as Sir George looked so bad, his face all drawn up like it was.'

He paused, and it was while I was wondering what line to take with him that Sanders came in with this report about the pinpricks on Sir George's right palm.

I didn't make any secret of it. Harlow heard our conversation, heard Sanders say that tetanus germs could have been administered via those punctures. So when Sanders had gone to report to Scotland Yard, I pointed out that someone perhaps *did* get at 'the master' after all.

'What d'you think, Harlow? Can you recall anything — any incident, no matter how small — that might help?'

'Well, Miss Lincoln, now the doctor's found what he has, I'll tell you what's on my mind. Just after lunch today I went into the billiards room to attend to the wines in the sideboard. At one end of the room there's a little passage leading into the greenhouse, which in turn looks out onto the rose garden. After a short while I heard the greenhouse door creak open, but didn't hear any steps. From habit, more than anything, I went quietly down the passage for a few yards, and there, just inside the greenhouse and behind a big flowering geranium shrub, stood the young master — watching George pruning the rose trees!

'His manner, Miss Lincoln, was suspicious, to say the least of it. At least, I think so, in the light of what's transpired. He just stood there watching, keeping well out of sight. At the time I just thought it was peculiar, and left it at that. I came back into the billiards room and finished my job, then returned to the kitchen. A little while later Andrews came for me with the news about Sir George.'

I made a few notes.

'You've been very helpful, Harlow. Can you think of anything else?' I said then.

He shook his head.

'No, madam, there's just that. I hope you won't mention my name to the young master in connection with it. We don't get along too well as it is, and I wouldn't like to lose my job.'

'You can rely on my discretion, Harlow. Will you send the housekeeper in now, please?'

I was doing the questioning in Sir George Anderson's library. Harlow withdrew and in a few minutes, Mrs. Roberts, the housekeeper presented herself. She was a good-looking, comely woman in the late thirties, with dark hair and fine colouring. I started off by asking her how long she'd been with Sir George.

'Nearly four years, madam.'

'I see. I suppose you're the — well, the baby of the staff, so to speak?'

'Oh, yes, Miss Lincoln. Harlow's been here twice as long, and Andrews — well, ever since he was a boy, I believe.'

'Indeed?'

I told her of Sanders' discovery and how we were considering the prospect of foul play.

'What's your opinion, Mrs. Roberts? Is there anyone you know of who could possibly have benefited by Sir George's death?'

'Yes, madam — *I* will benefit, for one. At least, I will — if the master's *meant* what he's told me several times. He's often said how happy and comfortable I made him and that he'd leave me a nice little bit in his will, if I stuck with him and looked after him right.'

'Well — it's very refreshing to hear such candour, Mrs. Roberts! I'm quite sure Sir George won't have gone back on his word, too. Can you think of anyone else who . . . '

I paused, watching her. She had a forthright way of speaking which intrigued me.

She hesitated for a moment, then:

'Well, there's the young master, Miss Lincoln — Master Vincent. It's always been taken for granted that *he'd* get most of Sir George's money and estate.'

I made a note of this — the young master cropping up again. When Mrs. Roberts had gone I had Harlow in again, told him of my conversation with her.

'Yes, that's true, Miss Lincoln. Master Vincent *will* get the house and everything now, I suppose.'

260

'Now, Harlow; if we had reason to believe that Vincent feared he'd *lose* all that . . . well, we'd have something to work on. See what I mean?'

The butler's eyes glittered.

'Yes madam. I do.' He squared his shoulders, looked me straight in the eye. 'I wasn't intending to mention this, in case you thought I'd a grudge against Master Vincent and was trying to make it black for him; but about a week ago, about teatime, I was passing by the master's study, and there was he and Master Vincent having a real good row!'

'Indeed?'

'Yes. The door was closed, of course, but I couldn't help hearing as I went by. It's not the first time they've argued; Master Vincent's a young spendthrift and *will* keep running up bills with the local trades people. Anyway I heard Sir George say: 'This is the last straw, young fellow. After this week I'll cut your allowance by half and by heaven, if you don't manage on it you'll never touch a penny of my money'. I heard that much, Miss Lincoln, as I was passing.'

'Y-e-es.' I pursed my lips. 'So you think that Vincent, fearing an alteration in the will, acted first . . . ? That he killed his guardian before he altered the will?'

'Wouldn't like to say that, Miss Lincoln. I'm just telling you what Sir George said. The master was a very hasty man, madam.'

'He was? I see. Well, thank you again, Harlow.'

The butler withdrew. I looked at my notes. What pointers there were seemed to aim unerringly at Master Vincent. I sent for him, feeling very pleased I'd saved him till the last.

He was a studious-looking young fellow in his late teens, with a mop of black hair and thick horn-rimmed glasses; a type that I invariably associate with fads and eccentricities; the kind of boy who, at school, would've been dabbling in fantastic experiments in chemistry or something while the other lads were out playing football. He stared at me with his dreamy, deep-set eyes and vowed he couldn't make head or tail of his guardian's strange death. For I told

262

him, naturally, of Sanders' discovery at the post-mortem.

'It seems a bit far-fetched, surely, Miss Lincoln. You're suggesting that someone crept up behind Sir George and jabbed his hand with a hypodermic needle loaded with lockjaw germs? I can't see it . . . for one thing, my guardian had no enemies, he rarely went out even . . . '

'Nevertheless, Vincent — the facts are there. In some way those germs were injected deep into Sir George's system. He would collapse in that garden and be unable to call for help. He would die a lingering and agonising death. There must be someone, surely, who saw — *something* . . . '

He shrugged slightly, walked to the window, stood staring into the garden. I waited a moment but he said nothing. I stood up, went over to him.

'Vincent — I've heard that you were at a spot very near to the rose garden — not very long before Sir George must have collapsed. Have you anything to say about that?'

He spun round. He was either a skilful

actor or completely innocent of my imputation.

'What nonsense, Miss Lincoln!' His dark, brooding face was clouded with rage. 'I went straight to my room after lunch and never moved till Harlow came up with the news about Sir George. Where on earth did you get such a ridiculous story?'

I smoothed it over. I didn't want any domestic complications at this early stage.

'Never mind that, Vincent. I admit I place little credence on domestic gossip. It is a fact though, isn't it, that a few days ago you had a rather serious quarrel with your guardian — over money matters?'

He chased a faint smile off his lips.

'You've been listening to gossip, Miss Lincoln! Yes — I admit we often argued over money. He expected me to manage on next to nothing, and dashed if I could see any reason why I should. Just the usual father and son disagreements, Miss Lincoln. Nothing more to it than that, I assure you.'

'Quite. I appreciate your point; but on these occasions you realise we look to the first person with a good motive. In this instance, yourself. You don't deny you gain considerably — financially, of course — by your guardian's death?'

'I don't deny it. It's common knowledge that I shall get practically all the estate, if that's what you mean. Still, I'm not so impatient that I had to kill to get it!'

We chatted a little longer, but I soon saw that at this stage I wasn't going to get much from him. It was dark now; and as we still had much investigating to complete, I suggested that Doctor Sanders (who had been put in charge of the case pending further developments) and I, stayed here for the night. To this Vincent readily agreed.

Later that night we sat in the lounge comparing notes. All in all, we agreed that Sir George had not died a natural death, and that our first job now was to find out how those germs had been administered.

'We'll turn the place inside out tomorrow,' I told Sanders. 'If we can find a hypodermic needle or something similar, we'll have cleared the first hurdle.'

So we left it at that and retired to bed.

265

* ★ ★

Next day we went over the house and grounds with a toothcomb but found no trace of anything that could have been the murder weapon. Harlow left for town shortly before lunch — it transpired it was his day off, and Vincent accompanied us on our search.

About four in the afternoon we sat in the library drinking tea. We'd almost decided to call it a day and get back to town, when Mrs. Roberts put her head round the door.

''Phone call for you, Miss Lincoln.'

The 'phone was in a little lobby off the hall. I went in, sat down, picked up the receiver. A gruff, muffled voice answered — flat, as though it came from a long way off. I recognized the symptoms. At the other end someone was speaking through a handkerchief!

'Victoria Lincoln?' the caller said. 'Listen — if you want the weapon that killed Sir George Anderson, search in Vincent Anderson's bedroom. Search *now*!'

Note the strong emphasis on the last word. Then there was a click and the line went dead.

I sat there thinking for a moment, then went back into the library where Vincent and Sanders were still chatting. I casually joined in the conversation, and after a few moments said:

'Vincent, what would you say if I said I wanted another look round your room?'

I watched him closely but his face was unperturbed as he answered.

'I'd say it was a strange request, Miss Lincoln — considering you went over it thoroughly a few hours ago!'

I stood up.

'Just the same I'm going to take another look. I think you'd better come along.'

So the three of us went upstairs, he leading the way. He stood around impatiently while we worked, obviously thinking all this was so much nonsense.

We pretty well turned the room inside out and found nothing. By the side of the dressing table stood a small green wicker basket — which I'd emptied on my first search. It had contained only a few crumpled up letters and so on — and a fluff of dark hair such as would come out on a comb. You know what I mean?

Right! I remembered this from when I'd replaced the contents of the basket after searching the first time. Now, that fluff of hair was on the floor again, almost behind the basket — which, to be candid, I hadn't intended emptying again.

Now I seized it, turned it upside down, shook it. The papers fluttered out — and then something shiny that made a clatter as it hit the carpet. I picked it up, noticing Vincent standing motionless, his brows drawn, watching.

It was an object about four or five times the size of an ordinary pair of scissors with a shape exactly the same. I turned to Vincent.

'Ever seen these before, young man?'

He shook his head.

'How did they get there? You tipped that basket out before — they weren't there then . . . '

His voice trailed off on a high note of incredulity.

'Well, they didn't *grow* there, did they?'
I told him. 'The obvious conclusion is
that *after* we'd searched your room you
thought you were safe, and hid them in
the basket. That adds up, doesn't it.'

He spluttered.

'What balderdash! I don't even know
what they are, apart from having no
earthly reason to hide the damned things.
What are you driving at, Miss Lincoln?'

I didn't like his bombastic tone. I
weighed the object in my hand and glared
at him.

'These, Vincent, are a small pair of
secateurs — commonly used by gardeners
for pruning rose trees and such-like.' I
made a sign to Sanders, who moved
nearer to Vincent. 'I think they'll tell us
quite a lot.'

I went to the window, held them to the
light. They were brand new, but the side
of one of the shafts was scratched badly at
one point. I looked closer. A needle point
was projecting here, the merest fraction of
an inch, but unmistakably a needle!

I held the secateurs upside down and
tried to look up the shaft, which was

269

hollow — but it was too narrow. So I asked the doctor to go downstairs for a pair of pliers and some wire. Vincent was leaning against the bedpost.

'I know nothing about this, Miss Lincoln — you realize that?'

'All right, Vincent. We'll see.'

Silence then, till presently Sanders returned. I pulled the needle out easily enough, and found it was indeed a broken hypodermic — the pointed end, of course, had been sticking out. I poked the wire up the shaft then, and in a moment had extracted a small piece of dried sponge. I held them out so that the others could see.

'That's how Sir George was killed,' I said, amid a deathly silence. 'The sponge was soaked with a tetanus poison — and the needle, when fixed in this hole, rested its broken end on the sponge. The slightest pressure on the needle point — and what happened? The poison liquid ran from the sponge, through the needle, and into the hand of the person holding the secateurs.

'Sir George died of lockjaw, caused by

tetanus poisoning; he was pierced in the thumb base by this germ-laden needle. See how simple it is.'

I held the secateurs in the ordinary way, as if I was about to snip something. The hole in the shaft rested against the bottom of my thumb. I turned to Vincent.

'There is sufficient evidence here to warrant arrest for the murder of Sir George. You needn't say anything now — I suggest you just come along to the police quietly.'

He shrugged. It seems he realized the futility of arguing in the face of my discovery. He said:

'As you wish, Miss Lincoln. I can only repeat, I haven't the faintest idea of what all this means.'

I said: 'All right, Doctor Sanders . . . let's be moving.'

We went out. I slipped the catch of the lock and banged the door hard.

I told Sanders to take Vincent into the library and wait there for me. I wanted a word with the gardener before we left. I went through the kitchen and there was Mrs. Roberts sitting at a table entering figures in a book. I told her what we'd discovered, and what we intended to do. She jumped up, her face white as a sheet.

'No, no, Miss Lincoln! I'm sure you're wrong — dreadfully wrong! Vincent loved his guardian — he *couldn't* do a thing like that. I — I — '

She sat down again. She was very agitated. I said:

'The facts are there, Mrs. Roberts!'

I left her staring at the table, her fingers tapping nervously.

I found the gardener in the potting shed. I pushed the secateurs under his nose.

'Ever seen these before, Andrews?'

He jumped back. He was an old chap with an incredibly lined face.

'No, ma'am — I haven't. Them's a pair of secateur's ain't they?'

'They are. Haven't you ever seen Sir George using them on his rose trees?'

'That I haven't, ma'am. The master used ordinary clippers. They're just behind you, they are — a-hangin' on the wall.'

'Then you know nothing at all about these secateurs?'

'I don't ma'am — 'deed I don't.'

I went back into the house. I stopped in the hall, 'phoned headquarters to ask them to get a set of fingerprints from the dead baronet. In the library Dr. Sanders and Vincent awaited me. Mrs. Roberts was there now, too, and as soon as I went in she started talking fast.

'Miss Lincoln — *I'm* the one who killed Sir George! I tried to be a nurse, and I know all about poisons. I fixed up the secateurs and gave them to him after lunch yesterday, telling him he'd find them easier for pruning than the ordinary big clippers. *I* did it. Miss Lincoln — I'm the one you want!'

I stared at her.

'Really, Mrs. Roberts! What exactly was your idea?'

Her words shot out like a torrent.

'Because Vincent is my son; my husband was killed soon after my boy was born, and I found out that he'd had a serious quarrel with Sir George — who'd threatened to disinherit him and turn him into the street!'

Vincent flung his hands out, shouting:

'Don't believe her — she's lying! She's just trying to protect me! Mother — don't be so utterly foolish! You don't realize what you're saying . . . '

He babbled on till I strode over and grabbed his shoulders. 'It *was* you, then, Vincent? You admit it?'

That stopped him. He gaped at me, stammering:

'Me? No . . . no, definitely not! I — '

'Then how d'you explain the secateurs being in your room?'

His mother was quick to jump in. 'I put them there, Miss Lincoln — after you'd searched his room, and before you'd searched mine.'

My head was beginning to buzz. I told her and Vincent to get dressed, we were taking them both back to London. Before she went out I asked her where she'd bought the secateurs. Without thinking, she told me.

'Stubb's general store, in the village.'

On the way to town I stopped off at the store, showed the secateurs to Stubbs, and had a little talk with him. When I came out Mrs. Roberts avoided my gaze.

'Tells me he sells quite a lot of these secateurs,' I said, casually.

She didn't answer. We drove towards London.

* * *

Doctor Sanders and I spent the next morning discussing every angle of the case. The result of our conference was that a statement was sent to the evening papers saying that Sir George Anderson's housekeeper, Mrs. Roberts, had been arrested for his murder. I can't say I was satisfied with this procedure, but what other course was there? For of our two suspects, she professed guilt, whilst the other, Vincent, denied it. In any case, I suspected that another fish would soon come nibbling at the bait — and we hadn't long to wait.

Just before six o'clock, a taxi brought the butler, Harlow, to my office — and we'd caught our *third* murderer! He came in looking terribly flustered, presenting us with a long confession all signed on the dotted line. All he could say was:

'Let her go; she had nothing to do with it. I'm the one you want . . .'

Briefly, his confession revealed that for some time he and Mrs. Roberts had been in love secretly. They'd planned to marry and live a life of luxury on Anderson's legacy after their employer had died; providing, of course, that Vincent, as holder of the money, looked after them satisfactorily. Harlow, however, knew he thought the world of his mother, and expected no snags from this direction.

Vincent, it transpired, had been taken from an orphanage by Sir George, where his mother had placed him on the death of her husband. She'd always kept track of him however; and as she'd always been in domestic service she'd managed finally to secure a post in the Anderson household.

Anyway, Sir George's threat to disinherit Vincent — overheard, you remember, by Harlow — changed things considerably. The butler foresaw Vincent, by his extravagance, making a complete wreck of all their carefully laid plans. So he decided to dispose of the baronet before he could alter his will, and at the same time to remove Vincent, whom he'd never really liked but who he'd decided to tolerate. For he knew Vincent would make the legacy over to his mother, who in any case would have had charge of things, Vincent being a minor.

So he bought the secateurs and fixed them up. He served as an orderly in the R.A.M.C. during the war — and had a brother in the Brenner-Munday research laboratory at Biggin Hill. So it's not hard to visualize how he came by the poison.

He waited till he knew Sir George was going to the rose garden for a pruning session. He told him: 'I saw these secateurs in the village, sir, and bought them, thinking they'd suit you better than the big clippers.' Sir George thanked him, took the secateurs, and started pruning.

Harlow watched from the pantry window. When the baronet was unconscious, he nipped out and secured the secateurs, placing the ordinary clippers near the body.

So far, so good. The next step is to make things look black for Master

Vincent. First he spins me the tale about seeing Vincent watching Sir George from the greenhouse.

Secondly, he plants the secateurs in Vincent's room. He did this just before he left for town on his day off; *after* we'd already searched Vincent's room and *before* we searched his. See how neatly it all dovetailed? Then as soon as he gets to Guildford he 'phones me, telling me where to search for the murder weapon.

He was a clever, cold-blooded devil and he conceived a watertight scheme which very nearly came off. Yet as usual, love conquers all! Mother love, in the first place. He hadn't reckoned on Mrs. Roberts swearing she did it as soon as Vincent's life was in danger. Just something, I suppose, that didn't come within the grasp if his imagination.

In the second place — well, as soon as *his* lady love was in danger, you see, all his craftiness deserted him. He could think of nothing save her safety, and blabbed out a full confession. Due credit to him for his sincerity towards her, anyway.

Victoria sipped her tea thoughtfully, and reached for a cream biscuit. Caroline tapped the rim of the cup against her teeth.

'One point I noticed, Vicky — you said you expected *another* fish to drift into the net when the papers received the story of Mrs. Roberts being arrested. Why?'

'Good girl, Carol!' Miss Lincoln's keen eyes gleamed appraisingly. 'Well . . . when I questioned Stubbs, the ironmonger, about the secateurs, he told me Harlow had been in a day or so previously to purchase a pair for Sir George!'

'So Mrs. Roberts innocently gave you a clue when she mentioned Stubbs?'

'Yes. She wouldn't expect me to check with him. She spoke without thinking, I gather, when she told me. She'd seen them in his shop and just blabbed out his name unwittingly, as the first thing she thought of.'

The young detective smiled softly.

'I found something else, too, Carol, when I searched Mrs. Roberts' room.

Another example of the importance of attention to detail! It was under her pillow — a letter written to her by Harlow, when he was away on holiday sometime, I expect. You see? No matter how carefully a murderer lays his plans, always these little unforeseen things crop up to spoil them.'

Carol nodded thoughtfully. How wise and wonderful Vicky was in the countless methods whereby the forces of law and order trapped the wicked!

THE END

THE FIVE MATCHBOXES
EXCEPT FOR ONE THING
BLACK MARIA, M.A.
ONE STEP TOO FAR
THE THIRTY-FIRST OF JUNE
THE FROZEN LIMIT
ONE REMAINED SEATED
THE MURDERED SCHOOLGIRL
SECRET OF THE RING
OTHER EYES WATCHING
I SPY . . .
FOOL'S PARADISE
DON'T TOUCH ME
THE FOURTH DOOR
THE SPIKED BOY
THE SLITHERERS
MAN OF TWO WORLDS
THE ATLANTIC TUNNEL
THE EMPTY COFFINS
LIQUID DEATH
PATTERN OF MURDER
NEBULA
THE LIE DESTROYER
PRISONER OF TIME
MIRACLE MAN

THE MULTI-MAN
THE RED INSECTS
THE GOLD OF AKADA
RETURN TO AKADA
GLIMPSE
ENDLESS DAY
THE G-BOMB
A THING OF THE PAST
THE BLACK TERROR
THE SILENT WORLD
DEATH ASKS THE QUESTION
A CASE FOR BRUTUS LLOYD
LONELY ROAD MURDER
THE HAUNTED GALLERY

We do hope that you have enjoyed reading this large print book.

Did you know that all of our titles are available for purchase?

We publish a wide range of high quality large print books including:
Romances, Mysteries, Classics General Fiction Non Fiction and Westerns

Special interest titles available in large print are:
The Little Oxford Dictionary Music Book, Song Book Hymn Book, Service Book

Also available from us courtesy of Oxford University Press:
Young Readers' Dictionary (large print edition) Young Readers' Thesaurus (large print edition)

For further information or a free brochure, please contact us at:
**Ulverscroft Large Print Books Ltd., The Green, Bradgate Road, Anstey, Leicester, LE7 7FU, England.
Tel:** (00 44) **0116 236 4325
Fax:** (00 44) **0116 234 0205**

DARKSIDERS

Mike Linaker

In twenty-first century America — a dark contrast of decaying cities — the Outlands are ruled by roving bands and Chemlands populated by mutants. Ordinary citizens are oppressed by money manipulators and daily violence. Marshal Thomas Jefferson Cade is one of a new breed of law enforcers. Teamed with his cyborg partner, Janek, Cade investigates the disappearance of Darksiders in New York. Then a female reporter also disappears. The case becomes personal and Cade must choose between love and justice.

HARDCASE

Mike Linaker

Daily violence, decaying cities, mutant-ridden Chemlands and treacherous Outlands — tomorrow's America . . . U.S. Marshal T.J. Cade and his cyborg partner, Janek, investigate a series of murders and discover a conspiracy involving a billionaire industrialist and military renegades with visions of taking over the U.S. government. Amos Sinclair is a powerful enemy, and has an army of combat androids doing his dirty work. In a high-speed death race, the bad guys play dirty. But Cade has something new to teach them.

THE BIG HEIST

John Robb

Duke and his gang pull off the big heist, believing it to be the perfect crime. Stealing seven hundred thousand dollars from an armoured truck — the monthly payroll of oilfield workers — the gang get clean away with the fortune in treasury notes. But Duke overlooks one thing: the bills are in denominations of fifty dollars and upwards. The serial numbers, known to the police, will be quickly traced should the mobsters try to use any of the money . . .